WANDERLUST
Book 4 in the Walker Family Series

by

BERNADETTE MARIE

This is a fictional work. The names, characters, incidents, places, and locations are solely the concepts and products of the author's imagination or are used to create a fictitious story and should not be construed as real.

5 PRINCE PUBLISHING AND BOOKS, LLC
PO Box 16507
Denver, CO 80216
www.5PrinceBooks.com

ISBN 13: 978-1-63112-157-9 ISBN 10: 1-63112-157-X
Wanderlust, book 4 in the Walker Family Series
Bernadette Marie
Copyright Bernadette Marie 2016
Published by 5 Prince Publishing

First Edition/ July 2016 Printed U.S.A.

5 PRINCE PUBLISHING AND BOOKS, LLC.

Books by Bernadette Marie

The Keller Family Series
The Executive's Decision
A Second Chance
Opposite Attraction
Center Stage
Lost and Found
Love Songs
Home Run
The Acceptance
The Merger
The Escape Clause
A Romance for Christmas (A Keller Family Novella)

The Walker Family Series
Walker Pride
Stargazing
Walker Bride
Wanderlust

Denver Brides Trilogy
Cart Before the Horse
Never Saw it Coming (In Production)

Aspen Creek Series
First Kiss
Unexpected Admirer
On Thin Ice
Indomitable Spirit

The Rose Legacy An Aspen Creek Mini Series
The Rose Dance (In Production)

The Matchmaker Trilogy
Matchmakers
Encore
Finding Hope

The Three Mrs. Monroes Trilogy
Amelia
Penelope
Vivian

Single Titles
Candy Kisses

To Stan,
From atop the walls of Lucca to our own front porch,
I love sharing the world with you.

Dear Reader,

It is with great joy that I share this story with you. In the spring of 2015 I was blessed to take a school trip with my two older sons and my husband to Italy. It was the first time I'd ever traveled abroad and it was life changing.

One of the cities we visited was Lucca and I fell in love! I knew the moment I walked through the walls to the beautiful city that I'd write about it.

I hope you enjoy the story of Gia Gallow and Dane Walker as much as I enjoyed writing it. And I hope you'll explore the world and see what wonders are there to enjoy—especially Lucca, Italy.

Happy Reading,
Bernadette Marie

WANDERLUST

Chapter One

Horses had a way of knowing when a person needed peace. Fairy Godmother was that kind of horse Dane thought as she stood in the middle of the pasture and let him take in the peace of the moment.

He was back in Georgia for another family wedding. That was three weddings in two months though no one had attended his cousin Pearl's wedding to Tyson Morgan. They'd were on a beach at sunset in Hawaii.

Pearl had every intention of having a big reception, but she thought a New Year's Eve party sounded like more fun, so she'd wait. He supposed he'd be back for that too. And he wouldn't miss it for the world.

Ohio wasn't his kind of place. His job wasn't his kind of job. Somewhere his life hadn't become his either.

He now found that he envied his brother Eric for getting married and staying at home on the land they called theirs. Their father had promised them all they could build a house there if they wanted. It hadn't seemed important to him then, but now he'd give anything to be home.

There had to be more for him than a miserable job and a lonely life, he thought. But now he just wasn't so sure.

There was the sound of a rider coming up from behind him. No doubt it would be Tyson Morgan's sister Lydia, who housed her horses at the Walker's barn. She always took a morning ride. He turned Fairy Godmother toward the sound.

With the sun to the rider's back, he could only see her outline, but it wasn't Lydia. A long ponytail swung behind the rider who was obviously new to the saddle. He wondered who had let her wander off. Eric usually kept tight reins on horses he lent out to new riders.

As the rider drew near, she waved. "Hello."

"Hi," he called back.

"Beautiful morning."

Her accent was familiar, but he had to think to where he knew her from. But the moment she came into full view, he remembered.

He'd only seen her once, and his breath had caught in his chest. Her image had stayed with him—her long dark hair that had a charismatic bounce to it and those dark chocolate eyes that twinkled. She might have stood all of five-foot-three, but her personality was enormous. Then, of course, her voice had run in his ears for the past two months. That accent still tickled his spine in a way that sent tingles down it, right to his core.

Yes, he knew her right away.

"Gia, right?" he asked, hoping that was, in fact, her name.

"Gia Gallow. You are correct. And you are Dane." There was no question in her voice. She'd remembered him.

"Walker. Dane Walker," he mimicked James Bond when he said it, and she giggled at his humor.

"I met you at Pearl's dress shop a few months ago," she reminded him.

"I remember." Boy, did he remember. He'd thought of her for days after that.

"I assume you're here for Bethany's wedding."

"I am. I guess if all my cousins and brothers keep getting married, I'll be visiting a lot."

Her horse moved rapidly, and Dane was ready to adjust on Fairy Godmother to help her out, but she managed to get the horse under control just as quickly and smiled at him.

"He is a fidgety one, this horse they call Mr. Melancholy."

"Mr. Melancholy?" he chuckled. "Eric gave me a hard time about my horse's name."

"Brother's are like that. I have knowledge that he named this one himself. I would not let him judge you on the name of your horse."

He eased back in the saddle. "I'll keep it in mind for when I need to pick a fight."

"Well, I only have another half hour before they will come looking for me. I told him I was fine to ride alone, but he worries about his horse."

"And the rider," Dane assured her.

"I need to get back into town and go to work anyway."

"You have the Italian gift store, right?"

Pride fueled that beautiful smile she produced, he knew.

"You remember," she said softly.

"You moved into the same building with Susan, Pearl, and Lydia," he offered as if to impress her with his knowledge.

"I did." She nudged Mr. Melancholy closer to Fairy Godmother. "Have you seen their new building?"

"Not yet."

"Will you be in town this week?"

He shrugged. "Maybe."

"Drop by. I would love to give you a tour of my new shop." With a wink, she turned Mr. Melancholy around and headed back toward the barn.

Dane remained in the pasture watching her disappear. The thought to ride after her only entered his mind after he couldn't see her any longer. But he knew it was a bad idea. First of all, riding up on her would spook Mr. Melancholy, and he'd toss her. Second, there was no need to get worked up of the beautiful Italian woman. He was heading back to the hell known as Ohio on Monday. He might as well forget about Gia Gallow.

Chapter Two

Dane rode back to the barn where Eric and Russell waited for him. They were rubbing down Mr. Melancholy, and his rider seemed to have already disappeared.

"I have a bone to pick with you, Eric," Dane announced as he swung his leg over the horse and landed on his feet.

"Me?"

"You gave me crap over Fairy Godmother, and you named a horse Mr. Melancholy?"

"Have you ever heard of a Triple Crown winner with an average name?" Eric joked.

Dane looked at the horse carefully. "That is no race horse. And you wouldn't have sent a new rider out on a racehorse," he argued.

"She's had the best teacher. I wasn't worried."

Dane removed the bit and bridle from Fairy Godmother. "You're teaching riders now? I thought you were strictly boarding."

"I didn't say it was me," he admitted. "Lydia taught her."

The thought that the riding instructor was Lydia hadn't crossed his mind. But he'd have to admit she'd be the best at teaching little women how to handle big animals.

He hung the bridal on the peg on the wall. "Lydia's still keeping her horse here?"

"Yeah. Eric said his grandfather has decided to ban them both from their property."

"Just for keeping a horse on our land?"

Eric shrugged. "The fact that his grandson married a Walker probably didn't help," he said referring to his cousin Pearl's marriage to Tyson Morgan, Eric's half-brother. "They think he's senile."

Dane would have voted for that years ago. Elias Morgan was one of the crotchetiest old men he'd ever encountered.

He'd never had to deal with him one on one as Eric had. Of course, Elias Morgan was Eric's grandfather.

As Dane unbuckled the saddle and lifted it from Fairy Godmother, he took a moment to consider Eric's bloodline.

They'd all grown up knowing that Eric's mother had been married to their father first. She had died, and their father remarried. Eric had never embraced his Morgan side, especially with the feud that brewed between families.

There had always been a battle between the Morgans and the Walkers. It had been handed down through generations. Dane had always been under the impression that the feud was over land rights. After all, his uncle had tried to use the family land to pay off a gambling debt. But it had started even before his uncle had made some shady deals, and Eric's mother had run away from home and married their father.

"Are Pearl and Tyson back from Hawaii yet?" he asked as he took the brush from the basket against the wall and began brushing the horse.

"They get back today. Just in time for some bachelor and bachelorette parties." Russell did a strange little dance that had Dane laughing.

"I don't think we have to work too hard to entertain Kent," Dane joked. "He's fairly straight laced."

"Those are the one's who let loose the hardest," Eric laughed.

Kent was an author of science fiction. Dane couldn't even imagine what kind of wild night they could have. He supposed they could rent out the theater and watch the new Star Wars movie. Then again, maybe that would only appeal to Dane as he was the only one in the world that probably hadn't seen it. He was sure Kent had run out and caught the first showing.

Eric walked up to the horse with an apple in his hand. "You're humoring yourself," he said to Dane. "What are you thinking about?"

"Kent's bachelor party." He looked up at his brother. "I like Kent, don't get me wrong. But when you think of Bethany the very attractive movie star and the nerdy sci-fi book author, you have to wonder why she'd choose him."

Eric shook his head. "You've never been in love. Nothing matters when the right person comes into your life."

Dane chuckled. "God, I never thought you'd talk like that."

Eric shrugged. "Some of us are luckier than others. You get to live in Ohio, I get to have Susan."

Dane's humor over the situation diffused. His brother was pointing out that his life was pathetic.

Fine, he'd take it. He was making good money even if he lived in a hole of an apartment, on a noisy city street, and ate take-out nearly every night. He'd been humbled by the experience. Now instead of driving up to the barn and riding his horse he had to make himself go to the Y and work out. If he wanted a homemade meal he had to make it himself, and he was no chef. When he was lonely, he had to call his parents or his brothers. They all had lives of their own, and they couldn't be expected to call him just because he might be lonely.

At this moment in his life, his brother was right, and he was lucky to live in Ohio—but Eric still was luckier to have Susan.

Once he'd groomed Fairy Godmother, he put her back in her stall and patted her nose. "Goodbye, girl. I'll see you tomorrow."

As he passed Mr. Melancholy's stall, he stopped. "You're a lucky man, aren't you?" he asked as the horse reached his head over the gate toward Dane. He ran his hand down the horse's nose. "Yeah, you know you are too. She's a beautiful lady." He chuckled to himself as the horse whinnied his approval.

As Dane made his way back to the truck, Eric walked out of the small office in the barn. "Susan's cooking tonight. Stay for dinner?"

"Could you sound any more like Andy Griffith with that drawl?"

"I still have a belt I could tan your hide with," Eric said with is an eyebrow raised.

"Wasn't your job to do so. But, yeah, I'd love to have dinner with you. Is that alright with Susan?"

"Sure, but she'll need you to run into town for some things," Eric grinned.

Dane let out a grunt. "You're using me."

"You're here," he said turning back to the barn. "I didn't want you to think we didn't appreciate you."

It was good to be home, he thought as he climbed into his father's farm truck and drove it down the road to Eric's house. Susan's car was parked out front along with Bethany's and Lydia's. He was walking right into a girls afternoon.

Never had he knocked on the front door of that house. It felt weird to do so now, but it wasn't just Eric's anymore. In fact, since the original house had burned to the ground, it wasn't even the same house.

Bethany answered the door. "Well, look who's here." She pulled him through the door and into her arms for a hug. "I'm glad you made it here for the wedding."

"I wouldn't have missed it for the world. Would have been here for your sister's wedding too had she not run off to Hawaii to get married."

"It was exactly how she wanted it. Did you get the mass texts with wedding pictures?"

"Didn't everyone?" He thought of the night they'd all come in. One-at-a-time. He'd been annoyed. Obviously, Bethany had a different thought on it. "Eric said Susan needed a few things from town."

They walked back to the kitchen where Susan and Lydia were both in aprons and covered in flour.

"This looks interesting," Dane observed. "Something break?"

"Hush," Lydia scolded. "She's teaching me how to bake a cake, and I'm failing miserably."

"You're doing a good job," Susan argued until Lydia looked away, and then she shook her head. "Are you staying for dinner?"

"Eric invited me, but looks like you're busy."

"We will still be having dinner."

"He said you needed some things from town. I guess that means he's sending me."

She smiled wide. "He's very good at delegation. But yes, I need a few things for brunch tomorrow. Pearl and Tyson didn't give us a chance to do anything for them before they got married. So, we're going to have a brunch for the family when they arrive home."

And that told him his agenda for Sunday morning was filled too. That's why one would take off a week to attend a family wedding, as he'd tried to convince his boss.

Susan's list wasn't too complicated. She'd already called into the bakery for the pastries she just refused to make. The butcher had an order for her, the florist a bouquet. And wouldn't you know it *A Touch of* Italy was holding candles for her as well. Why hadn't Gia just brought that out herself?

He supposed he'd find out when he made his long trek into town.

As he headed out to the main road, he stopped by his parent's house and asked his mother for her list as well. He knew she'd have one, and this would win him "best son" points in the end.

His mother, Glenda, had a stack of letters she wanted him to mail. "And if you're going to Gia's anyway, will you ask her to get you another bar of that soap I bought a few weeks back."

"She's going to know what I'm talking about?"

"Of course, she is. That's her business."

"Have you all become frequent shoppers there?" he asked.

"Since she's going to be in the new location with Pearl, Susan, and Lydia, we've been trying to be supportive. Besides, she has some of the nicest things. She's from Lucca."

He remembered her telling him that when he'd met her. "Inside Lucca," he added, still not sure what the hell that meant.

"Lovely area of Italy," Glenda added, only reminding Dane that his mother had once had a life before him and his brothers, and it had included some travel. She'd always said she'd had a wanderlust, and she'd satisfied most of it.

"Anything else?"

She gave it some thought. "No. Just make sure those letters get in today's mail, so they are postmarked today."

Dane kissed his mother on the cheek and headed into town on his unexpected excursion.

He laughed to himself as he passed the mailbox at the end of the road. Would they have asked him to make this trip if he still lived there or would he just have been another face in their day?

Chapter Three

The UPS man probably was annoyed with her, Gia thought, as he wheeled in his third load of boxes. But, he smiled as he handed her his handheld device that she needed to sign.

"I appreciate it," she said as graciously as possible as she signed the screen. "Hopefully, the rest of your day isn't so taxing."

He shook his head as he took the device back and pushed a few buttons. "I have three headstones in the back of the truck. This was simple."

"Headstones? Really?"

"You can buy anything on Amazon."

That brought a laugh out, straight from her belly. "I cannot even imagine. That is the craziest thing I have ever heard."

"Oh, I could tell you some stories. Have a good day."

She was still laughing. "You as well."

The man opened the door just as another man had reached for it. The UPS driver held it open, and the man walked through. This one she recognized.

"Good morning."

"Hi," Dane said as he scanned a look at her store. "Wow, you have a lot of stuff here."

"I'm building up inventory. The new location will have a few more square feet so I can display some local wares."

"Local? Lucca local?"

She smiled, and she could feel the heat rise in her cheeks. "You remember."

"Inside Lucca. Well, that's what you told me when we met, though I have no idea what that meant."

What was she to say to that? How could he possibly have remembered that? They'd only spoken twice.

"Inside Lucca means within the walls of Lucca," she explained to him as she had to hundreds of others who had walked through her door.

"Walls?"

"Nothing in America is quite as old as the places in Italy. Many Italian cities were built within walls to protect them."

"So you're from inside the walls—inside Lucca," he gave her a nod as if he might have almost understood.

How could she not just grin like an idiot at the man? "Yes, which would then be the older part of the city. The apartment in which I grew up in was five-hundred years old. It was a newer building."

His mouth dropped open then. Talking about the age of the architecture with Americans was one of the things she enjoyed most about her job. There were very few buildings in America that were older than the 18th century, and in Italy, that was just a mere few hundred years ago.

"I love old buildings, don't you?"

Dane shrugged. "Never gave it much thought. I'm fairly comfortable in knowing that I can have running water and a toilet anytime I want."

She chuckled. "My apartment had running water as well."

His nose crinkled up as if he were uncomfortable. "Susan and mother sent me. Susan said you had something you were holding for her. My mother said she wanted me to pick up more of the soap she bought from you. She said you knew what it was, as if you're only job is to remember what..."

"I'm glad she liked it," she interrupted his subtle bashing of his mother. "I just got a new batch in yesterday."

Gia walked to the small display against the wall. She never tired of the smell of the soaps or the candles. They always took her home in her mind.

"This is the one." She picked up the bar and handed it to him.

Dane held it to his nose and smelled it. "Yep, that smells like her. She's very feminine."

"As mothers should be," she smiled. "Is there anything else I can help you with today?"

His brows drew together and a small crease formed between them. "I never thought of giving my cousin a wedding gift." He let out a grunt. "Either of them. Well, to be honest, I hadn't been prepared for Pearl to get married."

Gia touched his arm. "She meant for it to be that way," she whispered. "I could help you with gifts for both of them if you're interested. I am very familiar with both of their tastes. How much do you want to spend?"

He frowned. "Is there some kind of code? You know a rule to follow on buying gifts?"

"Let me show you around my store and you can see what they would like for their homes, and you can decide what your price limit is."

What in the hell did he know about home décor? Dane's studio apartment was bare. He had one photo in the entire place, and it was of him and his brothers all on the back of a beloved horse, Eric standing beside them as he'd been too big to be up there with the rest of them.

Gia was pointing out small treasures from Lucca and each and every item in her store had some story that went along with it and the artisan that had created it.

"I enjoy these frames very much. They are made by a carpenter in Lucca. He carves each frame by hand," she said as she picked one up and handed it to him. "Look at that detail. Can you imagine?"

Dane found he wasn't looking at the frame at all. He was looking at her and was lost in her admiration of the craftsmanship.

When her dark chocolate eyes shifted from the frame to him, his heart squeezed in his chest.

"What do you think, Mr. Walker? It is a lovely piece. Bethany would adore it."

Clearing his throat, "You're right. She would."

With a little tap of her finger on the wood frame, she moved on to another shelf in the store. "Pearl, on the other hand, already has a home full of lovely things." She picked up two different items from the shelf. "These ceramics are also made inside Lucca, by an old artisan who is nearly blind. But the woman has been making them since she was a young girl, so she does not need to see what she is doing to make exquisite pieces."

He was lost in whatever she was saying about the plate and bowl in her hands. Truly, he didn't know anything about the stuff—he didn't really care either, but Gia Gallow sure did.

"Pearl likes nice things. Which one do you think she'd like most?"

The small grin that permeated Gia's lips widened. "She is very fond of this cheese platter," she said nodding to the plate in her hand. "She has mentioned it a time or two when she's been here."

"Okay. I'll take the platter and the frame and the soaps."

"I will wrap them for you. Shall I wrap your mother's soaps as well?"

He chuckled. "She'd enjoy that very much," he said, but he was sure Gia already knew that about his mother.

Gia took her time to make sure each package was as beautiful on the outside as it was on the inside. Dane handed her his credit card, and she finalized his purchase with some regret. She had been enjoying his company, but now he'd be leaving her store. That was a shame.

She loved how out of place he looked there. He wasn't built like his brothers who had the build of men who worked outdoors. Dane was cleaner cut. He looked as if he worked in an office, as he did.

She couldn't help but assume that the shadow of a blond beard was new and only because he was home and not going into an office. However, even his jeans were crisp, his boots, though they had a hint of dust from riding, were new, and his hair had been recently cut.

It was unfair to judge him next to his brother Eric in size. Eric stood nearly six and a half feet tall. Dane, she knew, wasn't even six feet, which she enjoyed since she hardly cleared five feet herself.

But he was nice to look at.

"How long will you be in town?" she asked as she set the bag of wrapped gifts on the counter and retrieved the box for Susan from under it.

"Till Tuesday after Bethany's wedding. No one else can get married for a year. I'm out of vacation time I haven't earned yet."

"I will never understand corporate rules. We Italians believe you should work and enjoy." She had to laugh. "Okay, that is what we tell Americans. The truth is my father worked from sun up till sun down and so did my mother. They still do."

"You are cut from that same cloth," he said, and the softness of his voice cascaded over her with warmth.

"They are proud of me." Though they didn't understand her need to not have her store in Italy.

"Why wouldn't they be?" The corner of his mouth turned up in a sexy grin that had her body temperature rise.

"Thank you, Mr. Walker, for coming by today. I hope they enjoy their treasures."

"I'm sure they will."

Dane picked up his purchase and the box for Susan, headed to the door, and the turned back around. She waited for him to say something, but he didn't. Simply, he locked his eyes on hers then turned and left.

Gia gripped the side of the counter and watched him disappear.

She'd been in America for three years now, and this was the first time a man had caught her eye.

She was no stranger to them looking at her as if she were some exotic prize to be won, but Dane didn't do that. What she wasn't used to was the way that looking at him made her feel.

Her cell phone buzzed on the desk next to her.

Glenda would like you to come to brunch tomorrow at the house at 10. Can you make it? Susan xoxo

Gia looked up and at the door again. Usually, she'd be in mass at that time, but God would understand that she'd been invited by the Walkers. God would know the importance of her spending time with Dane before he left Georgia again.

Making the sign of the cross from her forehead to her breast bone and the from shoulder to shoulder, she whispered, "Forgive me." The she turned to the small mirror that hung on the wall behind her, and she smiled. No man should come before God, but she just couldn't help herself.

I will be there. Thank you for including me. Gia!

Chapter Four

Dane awoke in his childhood bedroom with a start. As he sat there, a bead of sweat rolling down his forehead, he realized it wasn't that he'd heard anything to wake him—in fact, it had been too quiet.

The sun was up and warm as it filtered through the window and onto his skin.

He wiped his brow with the back of his hand and then tucked it under his head. He closed his eyes and thought about the room.

It was his and Gerald's room. Oh, if the walls could talk, he amused himself with the thought. They'd lived too far from town to have girls climbing in the windows, but they'd climbed out a few times. But once again, they'd lived too far from town to sneak out without being noticed.

They'd done things such as walk down to the river and fish by a full moon. There had been an enormous tree outside the window and during a storm it could be menacing and scary. But on a warm summer night, it was a refuge as the big branch came right to their window like a bridge to the outdoors.

There had always been two beds in the room. Sometimes they'd be pushed together for comfort, especially when that tree outside swayed in the wind. They'd also been the walls to some of the greatest forts ever built with blankets and sheets.

Long talks were had in that room. Some of those talks went well into early morning. They'd debated over Santa Claus and the Tooth Fairy. There were some very serious discussions over Super Bowl XXXIII. Atlanta's new team had gone to the big game under the coaching of Dan Reeves, and they had to play his old team, the Denver Broncos. It seemed unfair to Gerald, but Dane thought it was just. He'd been a fan of John Elway his whole life. If he thought back hard enough, he was fairly sure that when he'd taunted Gerald with Elway's win, he'd gotten a black eye. The thought of it had him chuckling to himself in the quiet.

Talks about football and fishing soon gave to girls and talks about birds and bees. He was grateful that walls couldn't actually talk.

No longer were there posters and drawings on the walls. His mother had redesigned the room, he knew, for future grandchildren. The room was clean of everything but a dresser and a rocking chair. The closet door, another menacing nightmare maker, was cracked open as the door was too warped to stay closed.

Some poor grandchild would be as afraid of the abyss of the closet as he and Gerald had been.

It wasn't long before the sound of the cattle caught his attention. He'd have to admit it was a much better sound than early morning traffic. Then he heard the roaring of the first pickup truck engine. Surely he'd actually slept through the first. The sun was up after all, and he knew his father and brothers were up before the sun.

Dane rolled to his side and pulled the blanket up to his ear. This was why it was good to be visiting. No one had awakened him and made him help out with the early morning chores. Suckers!

It was only a moment later when the door to the room burst open, and he could hear the sound of heavy work boots on the hardwood floor.

"Get your ass up," Eric's voice boomed from behind him. "You don't get off that easy."

Dane rolled over with a groan. "I'm on vacation. Bother someone else."

"You're home," Eric demanded as he pulled the covers off the bed. "Chickens. Get the eggs for mom."

"You have to be kidding me."

"I have a calf with an infection on their hind quarter if you want to deal with that. I'll trade you."

"Gerald, Ben, and Russ are nowhere? You have to bother me?"

He could see it in his brother's eyes. It wasn't that he needed him, they'd done just fine without him. It was that he was glad he was there, and this was the norm when he was there.

Dane sat up and ran his hands over his face. "I'll get the damn eggs."

"Good. Get a shower too. You stink," Eric jabbed as he walked out of the room.

"I think that's your boots," Dane called after him before falling back onto the pillow for five more minutes.

Gathering eggs wasn't so bad. It had been his job since he'd been six-years-old. Of course, once he'd realized that they were covered in chicken poop, he'd stopped eating eggs for nearly two years. Now what he wouldn't give to have farm fresh eggs every morning.

He'd opted to not taking the shower his brother had suggested. Frankly, he couldn't see the reasoning if he was going to walk through the coop and fight with chickens.

The basket he used to gather up the eggs had been his great-grandmother's. How it held up all these years, he had no idea, but it made the task a little more special, he thought.

"Glenda said you could spare a few of those," a voice called from beyond the gate.

Dane poked his head out of the door of the chicken coop and looked up at Gia high atop Mr. Melancholy.

"We seem to have enough for giving. How many do you want?"

The sun lit up her hair as it had the first time. She looked like a saint in that sunshine glow.

"I only need a few for breakfast," she laughed, and it sent a tingle down his spine. "I only have my jacket pocket to carry them in."

"You're riding all the way back to Eric's on a horse with eggs in your pocket?"

"I have done it before."

"What was your success rate?"

She laughed again. "I have made it most times."

Now he laughed with her. "I'll clean them up for you. Come back by on your way out."

Gia nodded. "I will do that." She turned the horse around and then looked over her shoulder. "Did we get your mother the right soaps?"

"They were exactly the one's she'd wanted."

"Fantastic. I will see you soon."

He watched her ride away, his breath caught in his lungs.

"She has to be one of the sexiest women I've ever met," Russ's voice came from over the gate.

Dane turned. He'd never heard his brother walk up on him. "She's nice."

"Nice? Damn, you've been gone too long."

"Just a few months," Dane argued as he went back to collecting eggs.

"Gia Gallow. Owns that Italian store."

"I've met her."

"And you just think she's nice? She's a goddess."

His brother's assessment of Gia wasn't sitting well with him, even if he'd have to agree.

"You going back to the house?" Dane asked as he returned with the basket and opened the gate.

"I have to help Eric with a calf."

Dane decided he'd had the luck of the draw with that one. "I'll take these in then. Anything else that needs to be done?"

Russell grinned, and Dane shook his head in protest.

"Never mind. Pretend that I didn't ask," he said as he headed toward the house with the eggs.

~*~

Gia rode back to the barn as the sun warmed her back. She'd never imagined she'd find solace in riding an animal as big as a horse, but she did. Eric had been very gracious to let her ride him nearly every morning. It was the perfect way to start her day, she thought.

Gerald Walker quickly moved toward her as she rode into the barn. "How was your ride?"

"Glorious. It is a beautiful morning, yes?"

He took the reins and moved to the side of the horse to lend her a hand. Luckily, she'd learned to get off fairly well. She figured that was why they'd let her take the horse out on her own.

"I'll get him rubbed down for you," Gerald offered.

"It's no problem, I…"

He leaned in. "If I'm in here then I'm not at the house having to help set up the brunch."

Gia nodded with a smile. "Well, and if I am not here rubbing down the horse, I can get to town and back before that brunch and I will not have to help either," she whispered.

"Sounds like a plan."

Gia pulled her keys from her pocket. "Can you text your brother and let him know I'm heading his way for the eggs. I don't have his number."

Gerald's eyes widened. "And which brother did you want me to text?"

She laughed. "I need to remember to be more specific when I am here. Please text Dane."

"Oh, the slacker got up this morning and had egg duty, huh?"

She shrugged. "I suppose so. He was saving me a few."

"I'll let him know."

She gave him a wave and walked back out to her Fiat, which gave her a warm, fuzzy feeling. It reminded her of home, though she'd more than once been told it was very impractical to be driving on dirt roads.

If she stayed in America longer than the few years she'd been planning, she would upgrade to something bigger. After all, everything in America was bigger.

The very thought had her laughing to herself. She wondered what she'd looked like the moment she'd stepped off the plane that very first time when she'd visited as a teenager with her high school.

They'd flown into New York. That hadn't fazed her too much. It wasn't much different than Rome. There were people everywhere and cars fighting for space. It was when they'd traveled to the Grand Canyon that she'd lost her breath.

Tuscany had some amazing hills and open space, but the wonder of the Grand Canyon—it still took her breath away just to think of it.

It had been her plan to return to America as soon as she'd finished her university studies. She didn't regret it. Okay, she thought as she veered toward the Walker house, she missed her family. Family was very important.

She'd go back and visit at Christmas. Perhaps she'd be very settled into her new store, and there would be no persuasion to make her want to stay in Italy once she went back. Last time, a month or so ago, she'd had a lot of restless nights in her old bed.

Her grandmother was getting older. Her sister was all grown and involved with a man Gia wasn't so sure of, but perhaps that was only because she wasn't there to approve of him. Her brother and his wife were having another baby, and Gia wasn't there for that either.

Then there was Marco.

Gia looked in the review mirror and gave the band holding her hair back a tug. The pony tail let go and her hair fell over her shoulders.

She didn't want to think of Marco, so why did his name and his face always pop into her mind? He'd betrayed her and then came back for her. That wasn't a true man. That was a coward, but—she let out a huff.

Pulling into the front drive at the Walker's house, she put her car in neutral and pulled the parking break. With her hands on the steering wheel, she took three long breaths and calmed her nerves.

Marco lived thousands of miles away with his money and his looks. No matter what her father thought, Gia was better off away from the man who could turn her head and melt her heart.

It pained her that he'd betrayed her, and yet her family still loved him.

As she reached for the door handle, she noticed Dane walking toward her car. Quickly, she took off her seat belt, opened the door, and climbed out.

"Nice car," Dane said with an approving hum.

"It reminds me of home."

"Little car?" He lifted his brows.

"The streets of Italy are not as wide as those here. Cars there are much smaller. You would not see one of your pickup trucks there."

He nodded. "Don't think that sounds good to me. I like my truck."

"You never know. Have you been there?"

"No."

"Then how could you say it does not sound good. Can you ride a bicycle?"

"Of course."

"Then you would be fine in Italy, especially Lucca."

He flashed a smile, and she noticed her breath caught again. What was it with him?

"Here's your eggs. Gerald said you were on your way, so I was watching for you."

"Thank you," she said taking the small basket with a cloth napkin inside protecting the eggs. "I'll bring this back with me when I come."

"You're coming for brunch?" his voice dipped as he asked.

"I was invited. It is okay is it not?"

Dane tucked his hands into the pockets of his jeans. "Of course. I just didn't know more people were coming. I'm a bit out of the loop."

Gia eased back and tossed her hair over her shoulder. "I think you fit in just fine. Everyone is happy to have you home."

"I'm glad to be here." He looked around. "I miss it."

"I had better get home so I can make it back in time. I will see you soon."

Dane nodded and stepped back as she set the basket on the passenger seat, then climbed into the little car.

He stood there, just beyond the hood of the car with his hands still tucked away, and watched her.

She took her sunglasses from the cup holder, slid them on, and then revved the engine, perhaps a bit too much. Quickly, she pulled the break and pulled away.

As soon as she hit the dirt road, she looked back at the house beyond the cloud of dust. There he stood still watching her drive away.

He'd be gone in a week she reminded herself when the thought about making a move on him entered her mind. Long distance never worked, and she wouldn't do it again.

He'd be nice eye candy for the next week.

She could live with that.

Chapter Five

Gia had the basket which had transported her eggs home, as well as the picnic basket she'd put together for Pearl and Tyson, both sitting on the passenger seat in her car. She'd even strapped in the picnic basket so it wouldn't bounce on the bumpy road. Inside were china and wine glasses, as well as some bottles of Tuscan wine.

The driveway at the Walker's house was full of cars, and she began to wonder if she'd misread the time. It was only ten o'clock now. Surely they wouldn't have started the brunch sooner.

Gia parked so that she wasn't inhibiting anyone else's exit. After a few minutes, she'd managed her way out of the car and loaded down her arms with the baskets. She gave the door a solid bump with her hip and started toward the house. Of all days, the wind had decided to kick up, and there was a hint of summer giving into fall in the smell of the air.

Gia certainly hoped all of the guests were inside the house and not paying any attention to her walking up toward the house with her sundress blowing. God was much too busy to answer prayers to keep the skirt down.

"You look like you could use a hand," a man's voice said from beyond the cars.

Gia looked around the basket in her arms and saw Russell hurrying toward her.

"Let me give you a hand," he offered as he took the large picnic basket from her arms.

"Thank you."

"This looks fun," he said scanning the basket.

"I hope they enjoy it. It has china, wine, candles, and some imported treats from Lucca."

"I can't see where you could go wrong with all of this."

Gia held down her skirt as she followed Russell into the house. The noise met her first and the sadness of it second. It wasn't the noise that bothered her, but the knowing that it wasn't her family making the noise. It was a familiar sound. Family gatherings were one of the things she missed most about Italy.

"I am not late am I?" she asked as they walked toward the kitchen.

"No," he whispered. "Everyone in this family is early. Sucks if you're having a party and get a late shower." He gave her a wink, and she laughed as they walked into the kitchen where everyone had gathered.

Dane wasn't sure why his coffee suddenly tasted so bitter. It might have been the way his brother was looking at Gia when they walked through the door, and she was laughing at what he'd said.

Perhaps it was because his attitude had been affected by it and there had been no reason for it. The way Russ had referred to her as a goddess still burned his ears.

He watched from a distance as she hugged a suntanned Pearl and kissed Tyler on the cheek. His skin warmed when she smiled. What the hell was that about?

Gia hugged Dane's mother and his cousin Bethany. Then they both jumped up and down in that girlie way as if they had a huge secret.

He sipped his coffee again. It was going to be a long week. Weddings made everyone act funny, he decided.

"Egg duty in the morning starts at six," Eric moved in next to him with his mug of coffee in his hand. "I'm glad my wedding is over. I don't know what to do with these women when they all start giggling like that."

Dane laughed. "I was kinda thinking the same thing. Yours seems to be in control."

Eric shrugged. "Oh, wait for it. She's too busy making sure the dishes line up. She'll be squealing soon enough."

And he'd been right. The moment Susan moved away from the plates of food, she and Gia were hugging as if they hadn't seen each other in a month. How was that possible? He knew, for a fact, they'd seen each other at least yesterday. With all the work going on at the building which they were all moving their businesses into, he knew they'd been spending a lot of time together. Perhaps that was why he was single and thirty-two. He didn't understand women at all.

Dane's mother orchestrated everyone through the kitchen, and they all managed to have full plates of food when they were done. She'd managed to set enough chairs and tables, strung together, to house all the guests. He'd seen her do that at Thanksgiving too. He could hardly find enough room on his little table in his apartment to eat his microwave dinner.

"Eric and Susan, you sit there," his mother pointed to chairs. "Russ, you there. Gia you there. Dane you there," she said pointing to three chairs near the end of the table which flowed into the living room.

"Let me take that for you," Russell smiled at Gia and took her plate.

"Oh, thank you. You seem to come to my rescue for everything."

"What can I say? I'm raised right."

Dane let out a grunt, which had both of them turning to look at him. He simply forced a smile and took his seat—after Russ pulled Gia's seat out for her.

At least the food was excellent. Dane t listened to Pearl and Tyson tell stories about their wedding on the beach at sunset and their honeymoon filled with snorkeling and hiking near the waterfalls.

It wasn't that he didn't like hearing the stories or the awws that came from every female in the room, but watching his brother lean into Gia, and her laughing at everything he said, seemed to be raking on his last nerve.

He took his plate into the kitchen for another helping of ham. He was a sucker for ham and tiny bagels. It was something he couldn't explain.

"Does your family do this often?" Gia slid up next to him as he tried to delicately pull two pieces of ham apart.

Dane looked at her then at the table of family members who laughed and talked over one another. He shrugged. "Yeah, I guess. Mom's always putting together a brunch or a dinner."

Gia eased her hip against the counter. "You seem uncomfortable around them all."

"Nah, just all the gushy wedding stuff I guess."

She pursed her lips. "You are not a romantic?"

Was that a loaded question? "Sure. I mean I can be romantic. I just…"

She laughed and rested her hand on his arm. "I am sure you are the kind of man who could sweep any woman off her feet."

Dane cleared his throat, only because he'd choked on the air he sucked in when she'd said that. "I'm not too sure I'm very smooth with the ladies. My mind has been elsewhere for the past few months."

She nodded and picked up the serving spoon to ladle more fruit on to her plate. "I understand. I still have some friends back home who will not speak to me because I moved away. I will admit before I left, I might have pushed them away."

"Why?"

She shrugged. "So I would not be hurt by leaving."

Maybe she did understand. "I get that. I think…"

"Did Susan make those little bacon wraps with dates?" Russ pushed in between them. "I didn't see them, but dad has one on his plate."

"Steal his then," Dane said through gritted teeth.

"Lighten up." Russ gave him a jab as he reached in front of Gia and grabbed the bacon on a toothpick. "Looks like I just missed them the first time." Russ ate the first one and then reached for another. "Did you try these?" he asked Gia, holding it up to her mouth.

"Not yet," she said as he clamped the bacon wrapped date in her teeth and pulled it from the toothpick.

Dane was sure he heard both himself and his brother sigh.

She gave them a collective wink and carried her plate to the table, now occupying a seat left vacant by Pearl's father who seemed to have disappeared.

"Could you be any more of a pig?" Dane finally took both pieces of ham and dropped them on his plate.

"Are you talking to me or the meat?"

"You," he whispered gruffly. "You're throwing yourself at her. It's annoying."

"And you're not, so I don't see the problem," Russ argued as he returned to the table.

Dane stood there a moment trying to collect his thoughts. How had it happened that he'd moved away, and the world went on without him? He was finding out, very quickly, he didn't like it.

Gia watched as Dane set his plate in the sink and disappeared down the hallway.

Bethany had a grip on her arm, or she'd have followed him. She knew what he was going through. He'd moved away from home, but the lives of his family had gone on without him. It was a familiar problem.

A moment later Pearl had moved closer to them and then Susan as well, and the planning for Bethany's bachelorette party took form.

"I don't think Bethany is supposed to know what we're planning," Susan whispered in front of Bethany with a laugh.

"I hate not knowing. But I do want to go out. I want to line dance. We can do that, right? I mean, that's okay, right?"

Gia bit down on her lip. "I do not know how."

"It's easy. I can teach you," Bethany gathered her up in her arms and gave her a squeeze. "That's what I want to do. And since you all let me sit in on your planning session, I think I should get a say."

Pearl kissed her sister on the cheek. "Then that's what we will do. How much trouble can you get into on a Wednesday night, right?"

And with that, it was settled. Gia smiled as she watched the women she'd grown so fond of over the past year, make solid plans. She missed her sister terribly, but she was happy to have been accepted into a family, such as the Walkers.

She looked around the room in search of Dane, but he'd never returned. Her heart ached for him. She had a week. Perhaps she could sit down and talk with him. They were kindred souls in that way. Maybe she could ease his pain and spend some time getting to know him.

Chapter Six

Dane sat on the tree stump just outside the chicken coop and watched the sun come up. His great-grandmother's basket sat at his feet empty.

He wondered if she'd ride today. Would Gia take Mr. Melancholy out on a Monday morning before she went to work to sell her gifts from home?

A moment later he had his answer as she rode over the hill and through the pasture behind the house.

She looked his way with that halo of the sun behind her. She gave him a wave, and he stood, walking out toward her.

"Looks like you've become a true horsewoman," he joked as he neared her.

"Some people go for runs. I think I like this better. Eric is very sweet to have him saddled up and ready for me every morning."

"I'm sure he appreciates you giving him a workout."

She lifted her head and looked around. "I just cannot think of a better way to start my day than to watch the sunrise."

And next week would be a sad one, he thought, when he watched the sunrise over the top of his coffee maker and out his tiny kitchen window. There would be no view like the one he had right now.

"It's going to start getting colder soon. You might think differently about getting up so early to drive out here. It's not like it's just around the corner."

She shrugged. "I suppose we will see how I feel about it. Collecting eggs again?"

He looked down at his empty basket. "It was always my job. Seems fitting that I still do it when I'm home."

"I have never collected eggs before."

"Come on down. I'll teach you."

"I think I will."

She kicked her leg up over the horse and jumped down. Dane had to admit she'd taken to riding like an expert.

He handed her the basket and took the reins. The scent of her hair blew by him on a breeze. He wondered if her shampoo came from Lucca too and if those flowers, whose essence now filled his nose, grew there.

He knew the horse wouldn't wander, so he made sure the reins were up and out of the way. Then he opened the gate to the chicken coop.

"Why were you just sitting there?" Gia asked as they walked in.

"Kinda was hoping you'd ride by," he said and then wished he hadn't. It sounded desperate.

"I was hoping you were out here too," she admitted and shifted her eyes to his. "I wanted to see you this morning."

"You did?"

"I felt terrible that you left the brunch yesterday and never came back."

He gave her a slow nod. "Was feeling a little out of place."

"I know the feeling. When you move away from home, you are focused on your life. You forget everyone else's keeps going—without you."

He found that he'd taken a step toward her, closing the gap between them. "That's exactly it."

She smiled. "Last time I was home I got into a horrible argument with my sister over the man she was seeing," she admitted. "They are talking about getting married, and all she knows is that I did not like him."

"Sisters usually can sense that kind of thing."

Gia shook her head. "No. It was not that easy. I did not like him because of who he was. I did not like him because I did not know him. I was selfish. While I was away, my little sister had a relationship without me. My feelings were hurt."

He hadn't realized that what he'd been feeling was perfectly normal. She'd pegged just how he was feeling, though. "It'ss as though they should have asked permission," he said, and she nodded.

"That is precisely it."

Looking down at her, her long brown hair pulled back, and her bright brown eyes looking up at him, he wanted to gather up this small woman and hold on tightly to her. The urge to kiss her was extraordinary. He wasn't sure how he had held back and not leaped at her.

"So, what do I do to get the eggs?" She looked around at the dingy area?

"You have to reach under the chicken."

Gia shot him back a look. "I have to what?"

He chuckled. "Eggs are under the chickens."

"Oh, I am not going to do that."

"It's not that bad, watch," he said as he reached around a chicken and plucked an egg out from under her. "Easy as that."

"They do not mind?"

"Sometimes."

"That is not reassuring."

He laughed now. "I'll help you."

He moved in close behind her, so close that he was pressed up against her. It shouldn't have affected her, but she was finding it hard to breathe—and that wasn't because of the smell in the coop.

He took her hand, covered it with his much larger one, and together they reached under a chicken and pulled out an egg.

"See. It wasn't so hard," he said with his breath in her ear.

Her stomach did a little flip as a tingle shot down her neck and into her core. She wanted desperately to turn in his arms and kiss him. But one other lesson she had learned about going home was that rash decisions weren't the best ones. There was no doubt in her mind that he'd kiss her back. They had some chemistry and that had been evident since the day she'd met him. But he'd be leaving in a week. There was no reason to get worked up over him.

Dane heard the unmistakable sound of another rider coming closer. He backed up from Gia.

"You get the next one," he said as he inched toward the door to see Eric riding up.

"Where is Gia?"

"She's learning to gather eggs," Dane called out. "Someone needs to take over my duties," he joked.

"I was just making sure she was okay," Eric hollered back as Gia walked up next to Dane with the basket and a small collection inside.

"I had never done this. I cannot say I would want to do it every day," she laughed. "I hope I did not worry you too much."

"It's my job to make sure my horses and my riders are safe," Eric gave her a nod. "You look safe to me."

"I will be heading back that way in just a moment. If I am not careful, the store will open late."

"That's the glory of being the boss, right?"

"Very true."

Eric turned his horse and galloped away, out to the pasture beyond the house.

Gia turned to Dane and handed him the basket. "There is one angry chicken in there that did not want me to move her. So I did not bother her. She is all yours."

"Thanks. Do you want a few of these to take home?"

Gia shook her head. "I still have yesterday's." She gently touched his arm. "Perhaps I can help you again tomorrow."

Dane swallowed hard. "I'll meet you here. Do you drink coffee?"

"Of course."

"I'll have some of that waiting too."

Gia moved toward the horse and then looked back at Dane. "I have a stool to get up on the horse at the barn. Jumping off is not as much a problem as getting up. Could you help?"

Dane set down the basket and moved toward her. Gia put her arm around his neck and his hand came around her waist then he gave her the boost she needed to get her foot in the stirrup, and she lifted herself up.

"Horseback riding is not for the short," she said with a laugh as she turned away and rode off.

Dane stood for a moment and watched her disappear. As the dust she'd kicked up cleared, he decided that he hated Ohio—if only he didn't have to go back.

~*~

Gia didn't like being late, but she had been. The UPS driver was leaving her one of those irritating *Will Be Back Tomorrow* notices on her door when she'd run toward him.

Luckily she hadn't missed him. Mrs. Small had an order she'd been waiting for in that shipment. Once she got that settled, Pearl had walked in with pastries and a tray of coffees. Pearl picked up a coffee, looked at the side of it, and kept it as it was obviously one of her fancy concoctions. She lifted another and handed it to Gia.

Gia examined the pastry, eager to bite into it. "You look like a beaming new bride," she gushed over Pearl.

"I didn't have this back yet from the jewelers, but look what my husband bought me," Pearl said as she held out her hand and flashed the biggest diamond Gia had ever seen.

"That is beautiful."

"He's a keeper." Pearl admired the ring again. "Let's talk bachelorette party for Bethany."

"I thought we did that."

"Lydia is on her way over, and we're going to do more planning," Pearl lifted her coffee to her lips. "Seriously, she needs something even bigger."

Lydia opened the door and raced in and right to the coffee tray which Pearl had brought in. "I have ten minutes, and then I have to head out. They are doing inspections today in the new hall. I'm a wreck."

Pearl turned to her. "I think Bethany needs a bigger bachelorette party."

"Bigger? As in more people?" Lydia asked as she tore apart one of the pastries in the box and bit into the small half that she took.

"No," Pearl continued. "More than just line dancing. I don't know. Let's get a limo, champagne, tiaras, sashes…"

"Tickets to Vegas?" Lydia joked.

"If we must."

"Okay, so you're just saying go a little more fancy and a little more trashy."

"Precisely."

Lydia gave her a nod. "Sounds good. Gotta go." And with that, she raced back out of the store.

Gia stood there, her coffee cup still poised in her hand as it had been when Lydia flew into her store.

"What just happened?" she asked with a laugh.

"Lydia and I have a system now. We just get it out there and deal with it."

Gia nodded. "A sister-in-law kind of connection?"

"Right. You have one. Are you like that with her? Your sister-in-law?"

Gia shook her head. "Not even close. There are times I think she forgets my name. I will give her credit. It could be because she is always pregnant when I see her. They will have three children by the time I get back there again."

"Do you miss home?"

Gia had to stop and think for a moment. "Yes. I miss my family and seeing them every day. But," she lifted her hands to gesture to her store, "I am surrounded by home."

"I think Dane is feeling a little out of place," Pearl said as she picked up the other half of the pastry that Lydia had left in the box. "I noticed he wasn't quite himself when Eric and Susan got married and this time, well, he's even less…" She bobbed her head from side to side as if she were looking for the right words. "It's as if he's not as friendly. Like he's mad that he had to come home."

Gia lifted her cup to her lips and smiled behind it. "I know exactly what he is going through. I realized yesterday, when he disappeared from the brunch that he is overwhelmed. There is this strange feeling, when you go back home like everything is wrong. You leave. You live your new life, but life at home keeps going on. You just do not think about it."

Pearl gave it some consideration. "He leaves, and everyone starts to get married."

"Precisely."

"We buy new buildings. Open new businesses."

"Plan weddings, or elope."

Pearl grinned. "Best damn thing I ever did. I don't know how those women do it."

Gia leaned her hip against the counter. "I always thought I wanted a big mass in the prettiest church in Lucca."

"Which one is that?"

"The Basilica of San Frediano. I will admit, not the most beautiful church from outside, but inside," she sighed. "I heard a choir in there one day as I passed by and even to this day, just to think about it, I have goosebumps on my arms." She held her arms out for Pearl to see.

"What if you married someone from here?"

Gia let out a sigh. "I never thought about it."

"Seems realistic if you're going to live here for a long time."

She was right. Gia had no plans to go back to Italy. It was nice to have open space and friends who were not related to her and the entire town. Being important to her community was lovely. And of course, she was very far away from Marco. If anything ruined the thought of going home it was knowing that he might also be within the walls. Considering the size of Lucca, that made him much too close for comfort.

"Well, I do not suppose I will be buying a wedding dress from you anytime soon."

Pearl lifted her cup. "Ah, but you will buy from me."

They shared a laugh. Gia wouldn't have it any other way, she thought.

~*~

Dane sat in his father's office, his laptop open on the desk, and his head in his hands. He'd wanted the full week off to be with his family and enjoy his cousin's wedding. Seriously, though, could the office not run without him?

He'd been fielding phone calls, texts, and emails all day long. If he didn't care about Bethany, he was sure they'd want him back right away.

To add insult to injury, they were sending him to New York next month to work. It was starting to grate on his nerves.

It probably wouldn't matter if he could work remotely from his father's office every day, but he was now babysitting employees of a bigger company—which he was in line to be promoted in, he had to remind himself. This was how it went when you were a top notch employee, but new.

"You're looking frazzled," his father's voice came from the doorway.

Dane looked up and sat back in the large leather chair. "Just a little drama, that's all."

His father walked in and sat down in one of the chairs in front of the desk. Dane thought he'd started to look much older since Dane's grandfather had died. Of course, there had been a lot of drama right there on the ranch in the past year too. He'd give it to his father then. Maybe he looked magnificent.

"I'm proud of you," his father said. "It's not easy to take on a responsibility like this and leave your family. Maybe one day you'll come back, but think about the experience you'll have had."

Didn't Everett Walker always have a way with words?

"It's a hard week. It's always hard to come back because then I want to stay."

"You're always welcome."

Dane nodded. He knew that. "I suppose it's harder knowing that Eric is married. He'll probably start a family soon, and I won't be here to mess up his kids."

They laughed. "Visit often enough that you can."

"Then with Pearl and Bethany getting married, it just feels as if everything is happening without me."

"I'm guessing the man that owns that company you work for started somewhere too. Get your feet wet. Make connections. Start your own company here in Georgia. You're young yet."

He sure wasn't feeling young. "I have to go to New York for a few weeks once I get back to Ohio. I suppose I'll add that to my list of things I *get* to do."

His father smiled. "That's my boy. It's all in the wording." He stood and took a deep breath. "I *get* to go to Elias Morgan's house and look at oil well plans."

"It still hurts to hear you talk about that man as if he's a viable business partner."

His father shrugged. "You can't hold on to hate forever. Besides, if this all goes well, maybe you can retire early," he said with a wink as he walked out of the office.

Dane chuckled to himself. He hoped it was worth all the pain the Elias Morgan has caused to his family to make the kind of money his father was talking about. But then it hit him. His father might have looked older, but he certainly hadn't appeared stressed. Maybe that came with the gray hair.

Chapter Seven

The sounds of a horse caught his attention and Dane raised his head to see Gia crest the small hill.

In his hands, he held two travel mugs of coffee, just as he'd promised he would.

"This morning is a little chilly," she called to him as she neared.

"All the more reason to drink coffee."

She stopped just on the edge of the chicken coop, and he realized this was the first time she'd ridden with her hair down. He'd miss this sight when he went back to Ohio.

Gia jumped, gracefully, down from the saddle and walked toward him.

He could smell the fresh scent of her soap again, and it was a fragrance he'd never forget.

Dane handed her one of the mugs, and her cold fingertips brushed his hand. "You need gloves."

She laughed. "I was told, by your father, I needed a helmet too."

Dane nodded. "Mine is at Eric's barn. You're welcome to it."

"I did not see you wearing one the other day," she said as she lifted the mug to her lips.

"That's why it's hidden at Eric's."

She laughed again, and that took the chill out of the breeze that had filled the September air.

"Do you suppose there will be enough eggs for me to take a few more today?"

He nodded. "There will always be enough."

Her eyes batted slowly. "That is very kind."

"I'd give you all of them all the time if I could start every morning like this."

A smile formed on her lips that warmed him from the inside.

"When do you go back to Ohio?"

"I fly out at the ungodly hour of six in the morning on Monday."

A line formed between her brows. "That is very early." She touched his hand. "I guess we had better make a date of this coffee time each morning. They will be over too soon."

There was no way to tell, but he wondered if she could hear the thudding in his chest as his heart was pounding so fast.

"Are you free for dinner tonight?" he asked without having planned to.

"I am."

"Would you be interested in going to dinner with me? Everyone around here is wedding obsessed. Maybe some time away from the house would be a good thing."

"That sounds splendid. Shall I meet you somewhere?"

He knew that tactic, and she was very skilled at executing it. If he didn't pick her up, she didn't have to have him take her home. The night would end on her terms.

"Chinese?"

"One of my favorite."

"China Dynasty?"

"They have the best dumplings," she said with her smile even wider. "Shall we collect eggs?"

"Suddenly this is my favorite chore," he said softly as he followed her into the chicken coop.

~*~

Dane drummed on the table with his chopsticks, which his mother would have smacked him upside the head for doing. So he put them down and sipped his water.

Gia was late, and he was suddenly terrified that she'd stood him up.

Maybe he'd come on too strong. Maybe she didn't like him and had taken pity on him. Maybe...

"I am sorry I am late. I was making travel arrangements and lost track of time," she apologized as she began to sit in the booth across from him as he tried to scoot out to stand.

All that did was shake the water glasses on the table and look incredibly awkward, but they both laughed.

Dane sat back down and wiped up the water that spilled over with his napkin. "So where are you traveling?"

"I made plans to attend a buying show and then decided to go home for Christmas. My brother's baby should have arrived by then."

He felt the words punch him solidly in the chest. The next time he came home, she'd be gone.

"How long will you be in Italy?" His voice shook, so he picked up his water and sipped.

"Two weeks. I think that will be long enough for me to embrace family, visit friends, and be ready to come back."

"Are you ever afraid you won't want to come back?"

Something flashed in her eyes. "Always a thought, I guess. But I chose to live here. I love it here, and my business is here. You know as well as I do when you go home you miss it."

"That's true."

"It takes about a week for me to realize that I do not belong there anymore," she said, and then held her hand up as if to protest herself. "It is not that I do not belong. It is that everyone has changed while I am gone and I have changed too. It is hard to balance the two."

He nodded. "I understand. You leave and come back, and everyone is getting married."

She laughed. "I imagine you have many more weddings to go. You have a big family."

He lifted his water glass in a toast. "To more weddings that'll bring me home."

She tapped her water glass to his. "And when you are here, I will assist you with collecting eggs."

The pain of her previous words eased in his chest, and his breath came easier. Gia Gallow would still be there when he got back.

Gia studied the menu. "Do you have a favorite?"

"Sweet and sour pork."

She gave him a slow, thoughtful nod. "I like that too. Shall we do that and of course dumplings."

He grinned. "Of course. And soup?"

"Egg drop."

"I think we've planned the perfect meal," he said as he closed his menu and set it on the edge of the table.

When the waitress came for their order, he placed it and ordered a beer, while she ordered wine.

"Thanks for coming to dinner with me," he said picking up his chopsticks and moving them from one side of his plate to the other.

"How could I refuse?" Indeed, how could she? She studied him as he fidgeted. His sandy blond hair had tunnels from his fingers having run through it. Though he hadn't done it since she'd been at the table, she'd seen him do it as she walked toward him when she'd arrived.

He was cleanly shaven, unlike this morning when they collected eggs, and she thought it made him look much younger, but both looks were attractive on him.

There was an awkward silence which fell between them until the waitress delivered their drinks. They thanked her, and Gia decided that she would start the conversation.

"Are you taking a date to Bethany and Kent's wedding?"

His eyes grew wide, and she was sure she had his answer before he spoke. "No. You?"

"No."

He let out a low hum. "Maybe we could go together. I mean we will both be there."

Gia lifted her wine glass and sipped. "I think I would like that very much." She set her glass back down on the table and pulled her cell phone out of her purse. "Would you like to see where I am from?"

She'd taken him by surprise.

"Sure."

Gia moved from her side of the table and slid into the both beside him. He quickly made room for her.

She set her phone in between them. "You have never been to Italy, right?"

"My mother has, but no, I haven't."

"Where have you traveled?"

"I don't have much to tell in that department. Ohio, of course. Texas. And the highway through Tennessee and Kentucky on my way back and forth to Ohio. Glorious huh?" He held up a finger. "Oh, but I will see New York."

"New York is fantastic. I dreamed of seeing it most when I was young. It was the first place I landed when I was a teenager."

"Why didn't you move there?"

"I wanted something less crowded. For the first six months that I was in America, I traveled the states trying to find the right home. When I got here, it felt right."

"You have wanderlust."

"Don't you?"

"Never did before now, but looking at your pictures," he motioned to her phone, "I'm beginning to think I'm missing out."

"It is beautiful."

"Very. I might have to visit someday. That is if I ever get any vacation."

"If you do," she looked at him, locking her gaze on his. "I'd be happy to show you around."

"What would you show me first?" His voice was light, and his eyes still focused on her.

"The wall."

He laughed now and eased back. "Wouldn't that be the first thing I would see anyway?"

Now she laughed in return, looked at her phone, and scrolled the pictures to a picture from atop the wall.

"The wall goes around the city. So yes, you would first see the wall. But we could walk the wall. It is only 4.2 kilometers." She watched as he did the math, or attempted to. "It is a little over two and a half miles."

He gave her a relieved nod. "And from there you can see everything?"

"Yes. When I am home, I walk, jog, or bike it every day."

"Did you always do that?"

She shook her head. "I did not appreciate it as much as I do now."

"I think your wanderlust is becoming contagious."

There was a part of her that hoped he'd let her take him for that walk. Suddenly she was homesick for an entirely different reason.

Chapter Eight

It wasn't even nine-thirty when Dane returned home. He'd been quiet when he snuck in the back door and very careful not to disturb anyone. The house smelled of fresh cookies, but they weren't on the counter, and he wasn't going to go looking for them.

As he turned the corner to go up the stairs, he noticed his mother sitting there.

The startle had him gripping his chest and his mother only smiling at him.

"I wasn't sure I could sit here much longer and wait for you," she said standing up.

"You scared me to death."

Her smile didn't waver. "How was your evening?"

"You stayed up to ask me that?"

"Word gets around. You took Gia to dinner."

"Yeah, so?"

"So I want to hear all about it. I made cookies."

He should have known it was a ploy. "You did that on purpose."

"I know your weaknesses." She rested her hand on his chest for a moment and then walked past him to the kitchen.

It was a ritual with Glenda Walker. When she wanted something from her sons, she'd get it. All she had to do for Dane was bake chocolate chip cookies.

He watched as she pulled down two saucers and two glasses, which she then filled with milk. She placed two cookies on her saucer and four on his. That meant she was digging for lots of dirt, he thought.

The each pulled out a stool next to the kitchen island and sat down.

"You don't play fair, you know," he said to her as he broke apart his first cookie. "You can't bribe me with cookies forever."

That warranted another smile from her. "I beg to differ. So how was your dinner?"

The sigh he let out as he dipped his cookie into the milk probably told her everything she needed to know.

"You like her?" she said softly.

"What's not to like? She's an amazing woman."

"Foreign and exotic too."

That made him chuckle. "Doesn't hurt." He took a bite of his cookie. "She has an understanding of what I'm going through. It's hard to leave home and live alone where you don't know anyone. I'm only a few hours away, though. She's thousands of miles."

"I suppose it gives her some comfort to have her store then. How wonderful to be surrounded by things that remind you of home."

He nodded. "You know, before I leave, if you made me a few dozen of these cookies, and I could freeze them, I'd be closer to home too."

She laughed as she set her hand on his. "If it would be of comfort to you, how could I resist?"

"I think it would."

She dipped her cookie into the milk. "So are you going to see Gia again?"

"I think we unofficially are going as dates to the wedding."

"That sounds like an excellent plan. You know, I could use a few gifts for my book club. Maybe I could convince you to go into town tomorrow and pick me up a few things. You seem to have excellent taste."

Dane leaned over and kissed her on the cheek. "I see what you're doing here."

She shrugged. "It worked for your brother."

He took another bite of his cookie. Oh, his mother was a real romantic. But she seemed to forget, he didn't live in Georgia anymore.

~*~

They hadn't made plans to meet at the chicken coop, but Dane headed that way early Wednesday morning, with two cups of coffee and two muffins, just in case.

This time, however, when he arrived, Gia was already there.

"I thought I would take in the sunrise," she said standing as he walked toward her.

"And? How was it?"

"Brilliant." Her accent made the word seem even more bright and exciting, he thought.

He handed her the mug of coffee he'd carried out. "Let's sit on the bench," he offered as they sat and he pulled a muffin from the egg basket. "My mom was baking."

"She is a fantastic baker."

"So this isn't your first Glenda treat, huh?"

"No. She brings the by the store whenever she is in town or stops in to buy something."

That didn't surprise him any. "She was bribing me with chocolate chip cookies last night," he admitted as he took a bite of his muffin.

"Why would she need to bribe you?"

"She knew we had dinner."

Gia grinned from behind her muffin as she lifted it to her mouth and took a bite. "And was she happy about that?"

"A little too much. My mother has a way of trying to set people up."

The grin faded. "And that is not a good thing?"

"Oh, it worked for Susan and Eric."

"Very well I might add."

Dane nodded. "She likes you. So she was hoping there was something to it."

Gia sipped her coffee. "You think she is wrong for that?"

He despised conversations like this. Inevitably he always said the wrong thing. "I don't live here. I don't know that setting me up is a very smart."

Gia took another bit out of her muffin, but it wasn't as if to savor it. "Right. That would be foolish."

"Right."

She sucked in a breath, and he realized at that moment he'd done just what he'd thought—said the wrong thing.

"I had better head back into town."

Dane looked around. "Where's the horse?"

"I decided just to drive here to wait for you." She stood and brushed the crumbs from her lap. "I guess I will see you at the rehearsal dinner."

And with that, she walked off.

~*~

Gia unpacked another box, but without the joy it usually brought to her.

She wasn't sure if she was more irritated at Dane for being an ass or at herself for even caring.

It wouldn't be the first time she got caught up in the flirting, assuming there was more than there was. She was mighty good at that. So why worry when it ended before it began? It wasn't a secret Dane wasn't sticking around.

She cataloged the new piece, priced it, and set it on the shelf which showcased ceramics made in Lucca. It was a brilliant piece. She'd ordered three of them when she'd gone home last.

In America, someone would probably think it was just a spaghetti bowl, but to her it was a work of art.

She took many things personally, like the bowl. It was handmade by a woman Gia cherished. The only unfortunate part was she was Marco's aunt.

Gia was taught early in life that you can't blame a relative for the actions and behaviors of others to whom they are related.

Her father hadn't spoken to his brother in nearly forty years. However, Gia had been raised with his children in her life and his wife, her aunt. In fact, they were very close.

As she unwrapped another of the bowls, she looked at the signature scrawled on the bottom. It was moments like that, when something simple like the sight of someone's name, made her miss home so much she thought she could lock the door and walk away.

But for now, the door wasn't locked, and that meant anyone could walk right in—and that was the case. When the bell above the door chimed, she turned to see Dane walking through.

Careful to set the bowl down in the wrapping she'd just pulled it from, she stood. "I did not expect to see you today."

"My mom sent me."

That stung a little, she thought but kept her shoulders back as not to let on.

"What can I do for Glenda then?"

"She needs gifts for her book club. She thought I could come by and get something for them."

"She did not want to come herself?"

Now he tunneled his fingers through his sandy blond hair. "She asked me to do this last night before I made you mad."

"Who says you made me mad?"

He cocked his head and lifted an eyebrow. "You're mad. I have a keen way of pissing women off by somehow just being me. I said things this morning that crossed a line, and I'm sorry."

Now her stance shifted, perhaps a bit too defiantly, and fisted her hands on her hips. "And tell me, Dane Walker, what did you say?"

She saw him take it as some challenge. He narrowed his eyes and fixed them on her. "I said that it wasn't very smart of my mother to fix me up since I don't live here. I discredited our friendship. I belittled you."

Being a strong woman, sometimes she found it hard to admit that she might not have won a battle with her strong will.

"So we are friends?"

Dane stepped only an inch further into the store, but it was progress. "Gia, you are a friend. You can tell a good friend when you meet them. Just because we haven't known each other that long doesn't mean we aren't good friends."

She fought the smile, but it won. "I am glad to hear that."

It was silly, she ached to hug him, but she resisted. "What do you think Glenda is looking for?"

He eased back on his heels. "I think we both know she only sent me so I could see you. She's counting on you to pick the right gifts."

Gia nodded and let her hands fall to her sides—the anger now subsided. "I have some ideas. Come with me."

Dane's mother had been right. He'd crossed a line when he'd said those things to Gia. Someday he'd learn how to talk to women. It hadn't been as if they'd established a full on romance. They hadn't kissed or slept together. He certainly wasn't thinking he'd marry the woman. So why had he said his mother was wasting her time? Because somewhere he believed it.

He followed Gia through the store as she'd stop and look at something, back track to something else, and then contemplate, yet again, something else.

"I think a small gift basket or bag. We could add a few items to each. What does she want to spend?"

He was sure he looked like a deer in the headlights. Again, why did his mother do this to him? He knew nothing about women—especially women in book clubs.

"I'll have to call her, I guess. I don't know."

"You call. I will put something together, and we will price it out."

She gave him a nod and went to work. For a moment, he just watched her flutter through the store. She had on a long lacy skirt that nearly drug the floor, and he wasn't sure she even had on shoes.

Her hair flowed down her back and bracelets clanked together on her wrist. She was a beautiful sight he thought as she lifted her head and looked at him.

"Are you going to call her? Do you need my phone?"

The accent snapped him right out of his trance. "I got it."

He turned his back to her and pulled out his phone. Best to not look at her or the distractions would take over.

A moment later he walked to her. "She says she needs four gifts. Maybe twenty dollars each? And she loved the idea of the gift bags."

"Exactly what I was thinking."

She handed him a shopping basket, which looked a lot like his great-grandmother's egg basket. "Hold this."

He followed her as she filled it with soaps and lotions. She gave a little squeal when she realized she had bookmarks. And she finished it all off with chocolate.

When she was finished shopping in her own store, she clapped her hands like a small child. "I might be a few dollars over, but I can adjust the price accordingly."

Dane shook his head. "I'll cover the rest."

She grinned and the dimple that winked at him nearly toppled him over. He'd never get her smile out of his head, even if he tried.

"You are a good son," she said as she rested her hand on his wrist. "Do you think you could do something for me? Run an errand?"

"It seems to be my calling this week."

"I would love a latte from down the street. I would buy you one too if you would get them. I could ring these up and have them ready for you when you get back."

He wondered why she'd send him away, but he wasn't even going to ask. It would only prove he was an idiot if he did.

"Sure, and I'll buy. It'll make up for the coffee from this morning."

She didn't argue. He handed her back the basket full of items and headed down the street to get coffee.

Gia walked the basket back to her counter and then leaned against it. She needed a few minutes to take a breath and gather her thoughts.

What was it about Dane that gave her such a giddy jolt every time she saw him? Oh, and how sweet was it of Glenda to think they should be set up. She should send her a gift too, just for thinking Gia was worthy of one of her sons.

She'd certainly been put off this morning when he'd said Glenda was wasting her time. She hadn't known exactly how to take it. Was she the waste of time?

Now that he'd come to the store, she realized that he was conflicted. She understood that. Long distance relationships sucked, but with Dane maybe it wouldn't be a full-on relationship. More like a long distance friendship. Heat rose in her cheeks when she thought that she'd like more than that with the man.

She shook off the thought and went to work making the perfect gift bags for Glenda.

Twenty minutes later the gift bags were nearly finished when Dane walked back into the store with two coffees and two sandwiches.

"I figured since it was lunch, maybe you'd like to eat too," he said as he walked in and set the drinks and the sandwiches on the counter.

"That was very thoughtful." She cut the ribbon she was using and began closing up the last of the bags.

"You did all that while I was gone?" He leaned in over the counter to take a look. "I can't even fold a piece of paper in half equally, and you took brown packaging paper and made bags out of them? Not to mention they are Glenda cute."

She laughed. "Glenda cute? What does that mean?"

He hunched his shoulders. "Are you kidding me? She does stuff like that. She uses ribbons and pretty paper to wrap up three little cookies. C'mon, just put them in a zip bag and give them away, right? Not her. It has to be a presentation."

"I knew I liked her."

"Yeah, and she likes you too," he replied with his voice unmistakably softer.

Gia took a gold sticker with her store's name on it, and placed them on each bag, in the back as to not take away from the recipient tag she'd added. She then took a bigger brown bag with handles, and a much bigger, more prominent gold sticker, and set the bags inside. "Here you go," she offered, handing the bags to Dane.

"She's going to flip. You just got me more best son points with my mother."

"I am glad I could help."

He didn't pick up the bag or move right away. Instead, he kept his eyes on her. "I'm sorry again for the way I acted."

They'd established that they were friends. In fact, he'd said you could tell when a stranger was going to be a good friend. She wondered just how good a friend might she be?

Gia walked around the counter and stood next to him. He was much taller, but she liked that feeling of having a protector, though she certainly didn't need one.

She rested her hands on his shoulders and lifted up on her toes to press a gentle kiss to his cheek. "You are more than forgiven."

His eyes were wide, and she liked that she surprised him.

As she lowered, his hands came to her waist. "That was nice."

"It was nice."

His eyes were searching hers, and she wondered if she were conveying exactly what she needed. She liked him. She really liked him. Friends were fine, but deep in her gut she wondered if there might be something more.

Dane took a breath as though he were going to say something, but instead he leaned in and pressed his lips to hers.

At first, she expected that he was simply taking the peck she'd given him on the cheek, just a little deeper, but she was wrong.

A moment later his hands moved from her waist, and his arms pulled her in closer as he wrapped them around her— his lips still pressed firmly to hers.

She inched back up on her toes and draped her arms around his neck, leaning into him.

His kiss softened and soon his mouth opened to her and he took possession. Her heart began to beat in the same rhythm as his—she could feel it from his chest to hers.

The protective grasp he had on her loosened as one of his hands moved up her back to the nape of her neck.

Dear God, he knew how to hold a woman, she thought as she sank into the kiss that was squeezing her insides tight.

Only the sound of the bell above the door had them pulling apart and the slight gasp from the man that walked in.

Dane winced. "Are you freaking following me?" he asked as he eased his hands from her and she stood back trying to ease her head from spinning.

They both looked at Russell standing in the doorway, a bouquet of flowers in his hand, and a devastated look on his face.

"Guess I should have called," he said gruffly.

"It is nice to see you, Russell. What can I do for you?"

"Nothing. I was just in the area and saw these," he said holding out the flowers. "I thought you might like them. They'd go nice in your store."

Gia moved to him and took the gift. "Thank you. They are lovely."

"I'll leave you two at it then," his voice shook as he turned to walk out the door.

Gia turned to Dane, who let out a breath. "I'll get him."

Dane went after him leaving her alone with a heart that hadn't quite stopped racing and a bouquet of beautiful flowers in her hand.

~*~

Dane nearly had to run after his brother he was walking so fast. "Hey!" he yelled, but Russ kept going.

Finally, he caught up to him and with his hand on his shoulder, turned him around.

"What's up with you?"

Russ shrugged off his hand. "Don't let me bother you. You were busy. Go back and finish what you were doing."

"What the hell are you so mad about?"

"Nothing," he said and hurried toward his truck. But Dane was right on his heels.

"Don't be an ass. What's wrong with you?"

"Remember that you don't live here, right? So waltzing in and taking the most eligible, most beautiful woman off the market is a crappy thing to do."

"I beg your pardon?"

"You heard me. I live here. She lives here. We were getting along just fine before you came along."

"Getting along? Are you telling me you're seeing Gia? Is that what you're saying?"

His brother looked away for a moment then back at him. "No."

"Oh, so you're just pissed I got to her first."

Russ stepped in until they were nearly chest to chest with each other. Dane didn't remember the two inches Russ grew more than him, but now he saw them.

"Don't worry, though. I'll pick up the pieces when you break her heart and go back to your little job."

He couldn't help it Dane shoved him against the truck. "I don't think she's a piece of property that can be claimed with finder's keepers."

Russ shoved back and even raised his fist to him before they both realized that Gia was standing there watching with a hand over her mouth and the bag of gifts for their mother.

Russ lowered his hand, opened the door to the truck, and a moment later he sped away.

Dane scrubbed his hand over his face. "Damn it."

"You forgot these," she said holding the bag out to him.

He took the bag from her. "I'm sorry about that."

"You have to go after him. You have to fix this."

"Fix this? He will be fine. He's a grown man and he doesn't need…"

She held up both her hands. "Fix it, Dane. You cannot let him go on like this. Especially when there is nothing to be upset about. The kiss…well…the kiss was only…"

He stepped in. "Don't tell me you're going to discredit that."

"I will not come between brothers."

"So you and him…"

"No. We are just friends."

"You said that to me too."

"Do not turn this on me."

Out of frustration, he pulled his keys from his pocket. "I'll go after him and talk to him. Can I see you tonight."

"Bachelorette party. You worry about Russell."

"This sucks," he groaned as he drug his fingers through his hair.

"Good bye, Dane," she said as she turned around and marched back to her store.

He watched her walk away and that amazing feeling that had been stirring inside of him when he'd kissed her felt like lead now in his gut.

The Lord giving and his damn brother taketh away. Maybe it had been a mistake he thought as he walked to his mother's car and opened the door. A few more days and he'd leave, returning to his miserable life, but with out such distractions.

Chapter Nine

Dane had set his mother's bag on the island of the kitchen and headed out to Eric's, luckily without detection. He'd managed to saddle up Fairy Godmother without having talked to anyone but a single stable hand.

"I think winter is going to be upon us soon," a woman's voice rung out through the barn.

"Sorry, I didn't know anyone was in here."

Lydia Morgan walked toward him with her riding helmet under her arm. "You seemed deep in thought."

"Suppose I was. How are you?"

"I'm doing great. Business is booming. All of them. We're all set to have Bethany and Kent's wedding in the new facility, so that's exciting. So, minus the fact that I had a run in with Phillip Smythe this morning, everything is good."

He wanted to laugh, but he forced himself not to. Lydia and Officer Phillip Smythe had had a hate relationship for as long as he could remember. To be fair to Phillip, she had the hate relationship. It was incredibly obvious that he didn't hate her at all.

"Did you get pulled over?"

He saw the color change in her cheeks. Oh, he'd hit the nail on the head.

"He knows my car and thinks it's deserving to pull me over every few months and let me off with a warning. I tell you, it's harassment."

He'd seen her drive. He was fairly sure that it was justified, and she was lucky to get the warning. "Maybe you should give him a break."

"You would think that," she growled before she let out a long breath. "Nothing a night of dancing won't fix."

"Is that what you're doing for Bethany's bachelorette party?"

Now she grinned. "More fun than going to see Star Wars," she turned and gave him a wave.

"I thought that was a joke," he called after her, but she kept walking.

The truth was, he wasn't feeling too well. Maybe he could skip the festivities tomorrow night.

~*~

Gia looked at her outfit in the mirror. Even though she'd lived in Georgia for nearly three years, she never could get over how she looked in cowboy boots. It wasn't her style. But then again, she came from a place where custom made shoes were well-made and sought after by the world.

The plan was they would pick her up at seven o'clock. She'd tried to convince them she'd meet them at the bar, but Susan and Pearl made it clear that this was the plan.

Looking at the clock on her dresser, she fixed the bangles on her arms and checked her earrings. Tonight she wore her hair full of curls and adorned more makeup than usual, but she was feeling a little out of sorts.

She should be embracing a night out with her girls, but she was still feeling the effect of Dane's kiss and the disappointment on Russell's face.

Hopefully, they were able to get things worked out. She'd quickly run back to Italy before she came between brothers.

A moment after she turned off her bedroom light and walked through the house, the doorbell rang.

When she opened the door both Pearl and Susan were standing before her with a bottle of champagne. "What are you doing?"

They both stepped back and Gia saw the limousine on the street.

"We are going in that?"

"Nothing is too good for our Bethany. So c'mon. She's the last one we have to pick up," Pearl said. "My sister and Lydia are already in the limo. We are going to drink champagne, dance, and laugh the night away."

Gia reached for her purse on the chair by the door. "I could use that."

Susan grabbed her hand and pulled her along as she closed the door behind her.

Quickly forgotten was the day she'd had and what was happening was the incredible bonding of *sisterhood* she'd needed.

Bethany twisted the top off a club soda the moment they picked her up. Then she began to top of everyone's glasses with champagne. Of course, she wouldn't drink. After having gone through rehab for prescription medications, alcohol simply wasn't something she needed to mess with.

Gia felt guilty lifting the glass to her lips, but Bethany didn't seem to think a thing of it.

"I've been looking forward to this for so long," Bethany talked above the music which seemed to have gotten louder. "I can't think of anyone else I'd want to have here with me than you girls."

"You are our family," Audrey lifted her glass to her. "I realize that my attitude toward you has not always been stellar, but you are my blood. You are my sister and I love you."

Gia saw the first tears of the night surface as Bethany pulled her in for a hug. "I love you. And I'm getting married!" she shouted with pure excitement.

Susan lifted her glass. "That's three of us. That only leaves three of you," she pointed out.

Audrey shook her head. "Right. I don't work regular hours. The urchins that are left for me are not worth it."

"He's out there for you."

Lydia put her arm around Audrey as if in solidarity. "I'll be alone with you," she moaned as she took a sip of her champagne.

Audrey let out a cackle. "You? Sooner or later Officer Smythe is going to pull you over and give you more than just a ticket."

Lydia's humored look turned to disgust. "Okay, this conversation is over."

Pearl shook her head and looked at Gia. "She's got her eyes on someone," she said lifting her glass toward Gia.

Susan scooted closer to her on the seat. "Details. One of the carpenters working on the shelves in your store? I saw them looking you over today."

"Pearl is wrong. I do not have anyone who I have my eye on."

She'd said it, but it was not convincing enough. However, it seemed to stop the prodding and just in time too. The driver pulled up to the bar and with a giant holler from Bethany, they all piled out of the limo for a night of drinking, dancing, and sisterhood.

The line dancing commenced the moment they walked through the door. Gia still wasn't sure she got the hang of it, but she was willing to try.

Bethany was hell bent on dancing until midnight, and it looked as if she just might make it. Audrey was keeping up better than anyone, but Gia had sat down at the table they'd managed to keep to themselves and drank down a glass of water.

"You've gone to water?" Lydia slid in next to her, obviously having had one too many beers. "You can't sober up now."

"I have to work in the morning," she yelled over Blake Shelton's voice which shook the walls.

"We all do. Of course, I can sleep in as long as I want," she laughed as she pulled back on her beer and guzzled down the little left in the bottle. "So was it Russell?"

"Was what Russell?"

Lydia wagged a finger at her. "The one you have your eye on? He's the cutest of the bunch," she accentuated with a nod.

Gia pursed her lips. "I do not have my eye on Russell."

"He has his eye on you." She laughed and sat back in the booth. "This is going to hurt in the morning."

"You should slow down."

"Your accent kicks up when you've been drinking."

And there she thought she was sober. "Well, it will be normal soon," she focused on the water and hoped that she would not hurt as bad in the morning as she was sure Lydia would be.

Susan and Pearl walked to the table arm in arm. "She's going to kill us with all this dancing," Pearl swayed against Susan.

"Sit down," Susan directed Pearl to the booth. "I'm going to get more water."

"You sound sober," Gia mentioned.

"I am. This is not my thing. These girls are going to be hurting tomorrow. I just hope Audrey doesn't have to cut anyone's hair very early in the morning."

They all laughed at that as Bethany danced her way to the table. "You're not all quitting on me are you?"

Lydia held her hand up. "Just because you chose sobriety doesn't mean we have to dance all night." She laughed at her own joke. "How come you still look perfect too? You suck. Your hair isn't even messed up. Or your makeup. You're pretty," she slurred as she leaned her head against Lydia's shoulder.

Bethany laughed and looked around. "Where's Audrey?"

They all scanned the bar, which had thinned out considerably.

Gia pointed to the corner. "I do believe that would be her. The one lip locked under the cowboy."

Bethany shook her head. "You can't take her anywhere. And everyone thought she was the quiet one." She turned and headed toward her sister, no doubt ready to unleash on the man who was working on a night to remember.

Susan looked at her phone and sent a text. "Okay, I texted the limo. It's out front and will pick us up."

Gia smiled as Lydia groaned. "I thought it was overkill, but I think maybe it was the best idea to have it."

She nodded. "These girls have had a rough year. I thought it would be nice to let off steam."

Bethany walked back to the table with an angry Audrey draped over her. "Let's go before she passes out on top of me."

"How was that guy kissing her?" Gia looked at her. "I do not think she is awake."

"I don't think he was either," Bethany said as she began to haul her sister out of the bar.

The ride home was not nearly as eventful as the trip to the bar. Pearl, Lydia, and Audrey had all fallen asleep, and anything Gia and Susan might have drunk over the course of the night had long sobered.

"Lydia was right," Gia looked at Bethany as she stroked Lydia's hair as she lay on her lap. "You look beautiful."

"Thank you. I feel so good. I have never, in my whole life, felt so good. I'm clean. I'm sober. I'm financially okay." She laughed at that. "I have the love of an amazing man. What more could I want?"

"I think you have it all for now," Gia said thinking that it sounded perfect.

Susan looked at the three women who had fallen asleep, and she leaned in. "Gia, seriously, who are the eyes for?"

"Oh, not that again."

Bethany nodded. "It isn't Russell is it?"

How could she even have this conversation with his cousins? "No. It is not Russell. It is no one."

"Dane," Susan said as if the name had just come to her. "You and Dane."

"There is no me and Dane." Not anymore, she thought.

"You're going to the wedding together. Glenda mentioned it."

"We were. But we will both be there anyway. It was more like that."

Bethany narrowed her eyes on her. "You kissed him."

Gia opened her mouth to deny it, but no words came out. That only sent the two women into laughter which they quickly muffled as to not wake the sleeping three.

Susan reached her hand out and touched Gia's arm. "You kissed him?"

She grit her teeth. She didn't want to discuss this. Nothing good could come of it. But these women were all she had right now. She couldn't run to her own sister and tell her what had happened.

Taking a deep breath, she closed her eyes and thought of the kiss. "Yes."

Again they began to laugh and quickly quieted.

Susan smiled wide. "I think that is wonderful. He's a great guy."

"I am not getting involved. I should not have let it get that far."

Bethany's brows drew in. "Why? What would it hurt?"

"First of all, he does not live here."

"Long distance works."

"No." Gia shook her head. "Second, it seems as though, maybe, Russell has some feelings?"

Bethany sat back and exchanged looks with Susan. "Did he tell you that?"

"He brought flowers today."

"What did he say?" Bethany asked leaning in again.

"Nothing. He did not say anything except he thought I would like the flowers."

Bethany wrinkled up her nose. "That's lame. What kind of pick-up line is that?"

"Well," Gia continued, wishing she weren't, "he walked in during that kiss with Dane."

Both sets of eyes widened on her.

Susan leaned in as Bethany had. "What did he say then?"

"Nothing. They both were mad and started fighting out in the street. If I had not gotten to them, I do think Russell would have hit Dane. I will not be responsible for that. I will not tear apart a family."

Bethany shook her head. "That's horrible. Maybe you could work it out. Maybe…"

"What is done is done. He will leave on Monday morning. I will go on with my life and him with his. Russell, well he was probably just thinking of a date for the wedding. I have no doubt."

The rest of the ride to Gia's house was quiet.

She offered to help get the other's home and to bed, but Bethany and Susan thought they had it covered. Lydia was going home with Susan and Bethany had promised to stay with Audrey and Pearl. She thought it was fitting that the baby sister take care of the older sisters for a night, after all, everyone had looked after her when she'd needed it.

It was nearly one o'clock when Gia walked through the front door of her house. It was eerily quiet, but she realized she was never awake at that hour. Of course, it was quiet.

Gia picked up her phone to put it on the charger and scrolled through the pictures they had taken that evening. She was glad she'd gone after all. It was exactly what she'd needed after such a strange and disappointing day. Even telling Susan and Bethany about the kiss made her feel better. She truly did miss her sister and her friends.

As soon as her niece or nephew made their debut into the world, she was going to head home. She needed a fix of family—especially now that she was going to have to forget about Dane for a while.

Chapter Ten

Dane sent Ben out for the eggs with the promise to fix the gate out in the far pasture. He'd never seen Ben so excited to trade jobs.

If Gia showed up for their usual meeting, he wouldn't be there, but neither would Russ. Ben hadn't mentioned having feelings for Gia, so Dane thought he was safe.

The gate, on the other hand, was a bigger job than he'd expected when he'd offered. Leave it to him to take on something monumental.

He was managing to lift the gate onto a two by four when a rider headed his way at a full gallop. He raised his head to see Russell slowing and swiftly climbing off the horse. Seriously, he didn't need this.

"Why are you out here? Ben is supposed to fix this. Not you."

Dane adjusted his ball cap on his head. "I traded. Now I'm fixing it. What do you want?"

"Came to help Ben. Don't think I'll extend the same offer to you, though."

"Suit yourself, but your attitude sucks."

He braced for something—anything. Russell was one to come at you with fists and shoves, but he didn't move. Dane went back to lifting the gate in place, and a moment later Russ began to help.

"I didn't know about you and Gia. If I had I wouldn't have shown up to her store looking like some love sick poodle," Russ admitted as he lifted the gate so Dane could tighten the hinge.

"And if I'd have known you liked her I wouldn't have been there."

"But you were the one kissing her, so I guess you win."

Dane grunted as he pulled down on the wrench. "This isn't a competition you ass. It's a woman. She deserves respect."

"And knowing you're just going to leave her on Monday, that's respectful?"

Dane gave the wrench one more pull, and Russ let the gate rest on the wood block. "No. And I'm struggling with that. The truth is, she won't see me now anyway. She refuses to come between us. We both lose."

"I concede. She's not between us."

"Doesn't much matter. Case closed," he said adjusting the fence one more time.

They continued in silence until the gate was good as new.

Dane pulled the cap from his head and wiped the sweat from his brow with the back of his hand. "Thanks for the help."

Russ nodded. "There's one more that needs fixing. I'll help you with that one too."

"Ben didn't mention it."

"Of course not. He's hoping to collect eggs tomorrow too."

They shared a laugh, and that felt better than wanting to punch his brother right in the kisser.

~*~

Dane was happy that the guys told him to meet them at a bar. He had seriously thought they were taking Kent to a movie for his bachelor party.

Of course, why they couldn't all drive together didn't make sense. Most of them would be heading home in the same direction if not the same house.

Perhaps there was more to the evening than he knew. Or Ben and Russ were just asses. That wouldn't surprise him either. There was no doubt in his mind that Eric would be skipping out early. Gerald probably would too. He wasn't one for staying out too late. Hell, Dane had barely seen Gerald all week. What was he working on that kept him away from everyone else?

Todd and Jake walked into the bar together with Kent in tow. Dane supposed they were all bonding now. The only one left was Tyson, and just as he'd thought it, Tyson walked in.

Jake eyed the waitress as she moved toward him and cozied up to him. "Hey, sugar, haven't seen you in a while. Where ya been hiding?"

"Working on the race car."

"I do love that car," she said giving him a wink. She then turned her attention to the men who had gathered around the two high-topped tables. "What can I get you, boys?"

Each of them ordered their favorite beer, and she quietly listened and never wrote a single one down. With a nod, she looked right at Kent. "You the one marrying the movie star?"

His eyes grew wide, and he coughed nervously. "Former movie star. She's writing children's books now."

She smiled. "She did good. You're a looker."

Dane watched as Kent processed that as the waitress walked away. He didn't know why Kent would be so surprised. Sure, Bethany was his cousin, but any warm blooded man could see she was a classic Hollywood beauty.

What didn't surprise him was that Jake knew her. Jake knew every good looking woman. He wasn't sure what it was that made him so attractive to the opposite sex, except for the fact that he raced cars, and that seemed to be a conversation starter. Telling someone you were a software developer, didn't exactly turn on women. However, Gia hadn't seemed turned off by it.

He realized he was the only one not partaking in conversation as the waitress returned with a tray of beers.

She tucked the tray up under her arm. "You boys in here for the show?"

Kent's eyes opened wide. "Show?"

The waitress grinned. "You boys keeping secrets?"

Jake, Todd, and even Eric grinned. They'd planned something more than just drinks.

Dane looked round the bar and realized that it was incredibly full for a Thursday evening. "What did you guys bring us in on?"

Jake took a long sip of his beer. "C'mon, it's a bachelor party. It's time to enjoy the single life and looking at some lovely ladies."

"Lovely ladies?" Kent asked, and Jake nodded. Kent's face grew pale. "I didn't know this was what we were doing," he said as if he were apologizing to Dane.

Dane lifted his beer and tapped it to Kent's. "Might as well enjoy it. They're right. This is what bachelor parties are all about."

~*~

By the time Dane crawled into his childhood bed, his head had stopped swimming. Worse, he'd have to head into town to pick up his mother's car. She wasn't going to be very happy about that, but he'd needed to let off some steam, and he had.

The pounding on the door was no doubt Russell he thought as he pulled the pillow out from under his head and put it over his face as the door flew open.

"I've got just enough time to haul your butt to town to get Mom's car and get you back before she realizes you were too drunk to drive it home," he shouted as he pulled the pillow from Dane's head. "She still doesn't like knowing her baby boys drink."

"We are grown men all over the drinking age."

"Yeah, and she's still mom."

That was true enough. She didn't mind them drinking, but she did have a fit when they tied one on.

Dane kicked his feet over the side of the bed and forced himself to sit up. "I'll be down in ten."

"Five. I got crap to do today," he shouted again, most assuredly on purpose, as he left the room.

Gravity was fighting to pull Dane back down to the pillow, but he forced himself up and walked to the bathroom.

An hour later Russell was driving away as Dane walked to his mother's car. He had the urge to drive toward Gia's store and poke his head in. Would she believe he was there to buy his mother something?

He unlocked the car, opened the door, and sunk into the seat. No. She'd made herself clear. He needed to respect that. Besides, he'd see her at the wedding on Saturday and then he'd be gone by Monday. If he truly respected her, then he needed to respect her wishes.

Suddenly, Monday couldn't come quick enough.

~*~

Gia watched Dane sit in Glenda's car in the parking lot of the bar in which they'd gone to last night. She'd seen the car when she'd gone to the bakery and then saw Russell pull up and drop Dane off.

She clutched the bag with her muffin in it in her hand as she stared out the window. Why hadn't he driven away? Was something wrong? Should she help him?

But she didn't move. Everything inside of her wanted to go to him, but she'd been very specific about how she'd felt.

At least it was a good sign that Russell had driven him into town. Perhaps that meant he'd taken him home and taken care of him too.

That was the whole point behind Gia telling them she wouldn't get between them. It had worked. They were mended. She'd done what was right, but as she leaned against the window, she felt the loneliness of what she'd done. She'd give nearly anything for another kiss from Dane.

A few moments later, Dane pulled out of the parking lot and headed out of town. She'd been hopeful that maybe he'd drive toward her store. And she was foolish enough to know she'd run back over too.

This was better she forced herself to believe as she walked out to the street. Whatever momentary crush she'd had on Dane Walker, it had to be over.

Chapter Eleven

Gia set aside extra time Saturday morning to wrap up the gift she'd had flown in for Bethany and Kent. There was a family in Lucca that made blown glass. She'd gone to school with one of their sons and had always appreciated the skill involved in such an art. The stemware she'd ordered from them had only arrived on Thursday. She hadn't been so sure they were going to make it.

Wrapping gifts was one of Gia's favorite parts of her job. It was glorious to make something so tempting and gorgeous before the actual gift was even revealed.

She'd chosen a handmade tablecloth, from Lucca of course, as the wrapping. Then she tied it up with ribbons of silk and lace, then added fresh cut flowers she'd purchased at the florist on her way into work.

The wedding wasn't until five o'clock. She had plenty of time to clean the store and make it home to get dressed for the wedding. It would be the first venue in the new building which Lydia and Pearl had purchased as their Wedding Mecca. She laughed at the name they'd given it in reference. It had a bridal store, a florist, a reception hall, and she'd heard that a photographer was moving in as well. Lydia's store would be the next to open. The contractors only had a few more items to finish up and then she could start packing up. Before she headed back to Lucca for Christmas, she'd be moved to her new location.

Gia stepped back and looked at her creation. She certainly had a knack for making something ordinary, such as a table cloth, look miraculous. Her mother had always said she'd had a gift for such.

~*~

Dane paced outside the church in the tuxedo Bethany was making him wear. He wasn't standing up with the groom, so why in the hell did he have to wear the monkey suit? Because he was an usher, he could hear his mother's voice ringing in his ear.

This was worse than being a groom's man as he'd been in his brother Eric's wedding to Susan. Now he had to talk to each of the guests and escort them down the aisle.

Seriously, he'd rather just sit in the back, watch his cousin get married, and then sulk by the cash bar after. Was that too much to ask?

Gerald walked out the front doors of the church tugging on the sleeves of his tuxedo. "I swear that girl Sunshine, who works for Pearl, purposely got my jacket too short."

"Why would she do that?"

"I made a pass at her, and she's married."

That caused Dane to chuckle. Perhaps she had then.

Gerald adjusted the jacket once more. "Why are you standing out here? Waiting for customers?" he joked.

"Fresh air. I'm very quickly getting over the wedding thing."

"Audrey is the only girl cousin left to get married right? She's not seeing anyone. Todd and Jake don't care about getting married, right? We're safe for a bit? "

Dane chuckled. "You'd think so. But with this family, suddenly, I don't know. I'm worried Mom will want to renew her vows just to have a reception in Lydia's new hall."

He saw his brother's face go pale. "Dear God, she wouldn't really do that would she?"

"Oh, I think she would."

The first cars began to pull into the parking lot, and Dane could already feel his stomach tighten.

It was time to buck up and be a man. One of those guests would soon be Gia, and it would be the first time he'd see her since she friend listed him and his brother.

The church was filling, and Dane had walked at least twenty people he didn't know to their seats. How big was Kent's family? And for Kent being a man of few words, his grandmother made up for that. Dane's back had a kink in it from hunching over to listen to the soft voice of the woman as they walked as slow as the bride would down the aisle. But in the end, she'd patted his cheek and kissed him. Perhaps that was the best part of the day, in hindsight.

As he headed back down the aisle, he saw Russell offer his arm to Gia. They walked toward him as he stopped in the aisle to let them pass.

She kept her eyes on the ground and that curt little move sliced right through him. Fine, if she couldn't even lift her eyes and smile at him, perhaps that little friendship they'd discussed wasn't really a thing.

That stupid early morning flight on Monday morning wasn't going to arrive early enough he thought as he plastered a forced smile to his lips to escort another of Kent's family members, and there must have been a hundred of them, down the aisle.

Gia smiled at Russell and gave his hand a gentle squeeze as she took her seat.

She'd averted her attention from Dane as she'd seen him walking toward her. It was childish, but she couldn't help herself. Her heart was racing so fast in her chest she was sure it could burst through. She'd contemplated walking in late, but that wasn't fair to Bethany, who had grown to be a dear friend. This wasn't about her and Dane. It was Bethany and Kent's wedding. Bethany had been through enough. She didn't need Gia's petty feelings to get in the way of her big day.

The small church was filled, and the music began. Gia pulled a tissue from her small clutch, as she knew she'd be needing it. She always cried at weddings, especially at weddings of friends.

Audrey walked down the aisle first followed by Pearl and then Kent's niece and nephew, who were being followed by their mother, Kent's sister. Small laughs erupted from the guests as she tried to guide her young children the few feet to the alter where their father waited for them.

Then Bethany and her father emerged from the doorway, and the guests stood.

Gia's tears started the moment they began to walk toward the alter and Bethany's eye were fixed on Kent's. And was her father tearing up?

Gia wiped her eyes. This was a big moment for Bethany. Her father had been missing from her life for so many years and had had to think about walking her down the aisle.

He'd finally agreed, and it seemed to have moved him.

She hated to cry in public. She never looked good after a cry. Her nose and cheeks would redden, and her eyes would then swell. Oh, what the hell, who did she have to impress. She turned away the only man that had made her feel alive in years.

As Bethany reached the alter, Byron Walker lifted her veil and kissed her cheek. Then he hugged Kent, and it was obviously unscripted as it caused Kent to burst into tears.

Glenda waved a tissue at him, and he took it to wipe his eyes.

The mister started the ceremony, and the guests took their seats. But as Gia turned slightly to move her clutch from the seat, she caught Dane's eye. That flash, that moment was theirs. What had she done? She very well could have fallen in love with the man, but she'd turned him away.

She sat quickly and gripped tightly to the clutch on her lap. In a few days, he'd be gone. That was the point. She'd forget him in time.

But as the ceremony continued and the vows of love were spoken, Gia wasn't sure she'd ever forget him fully— or that kiss. She squeezed her eyes closed and prayed for the pain to go away. She would not become a pawn between two brothers and the cause for them to fight. She'd seen it happen. She'd seen it tear an entire family apart. It wouldn't happen because of her—never.

Dane walked up the aisle and sat down next to his parents in the pew. Russell slid in next to him.

They'd exchanged looks, and a lot was said in that instant, he thought. Every muscle in his body had begun to shake. It was only attraction. He knew that. She was one helluva looker and a damn good kisser. He liked women with a head full of smarts too. Gia Gallow was the package.

Russell gave him an elbow to the arm and a nod toward Kent. Dane looked up to see the man sobbing and Bethany reaching up to wipe his tears. Dane couldn't imagine a man crying at a wedding, especially his own. Sure, he'd like to settle down someday, but he didn't suppose he'd be that emotional. It wasn't as if Kent embraced the single life that was for sure. He usually was hold up in some hotel room writing. Maybe that was what made the moment sad. He'd never be alone in that hotel room again.

The thoughts he was having made Dane realize that he was shallow. Love was an amazing drug. His parents were high with it, and he'd seen Eric fall to its mercy. No doubt Kent was a victim, and it went far beyond his wife's beauty.

He'd seen her at her lowest and ugliest times, and yet he'd waited, and now they were there getting married.

He felt the sting of a tear burn his eye, and he batted it away, but it continued. Damn! He was fighting a losing battle.

A tear streaked down his cheek, and he quickly wiped it clean, but not before Russell noticed.

"Really?" he whispered and Dane made sure to jab his elbow into Russell's side hard enough, this time, it made him wince.

This was stupid. This wasn't even his wedding, why was he crying like some girl?

His mother slid him a tissue and patted his hand as she gave him a gentle smile. That did it. Now he was sobbing. He hadn't cried since he wrecked his brother's motorcycle on the dirt road behind the house. He'd needed six stitches and at least twenty bandages over his body that day. There had been dirt ground deep inside wounds, and even then, he'd only shed a few tears. He'd been fifteen-years-old. What the hell was making him cry?

The worst mistake he'd made was turning his head to look at the pew behind him and across the aisle. The moment he did so, Gia's eyes lifted, and her tear soaked cheeks matched his. Again, they'd connected, and there was a near searing burn in his chest.

Screw Russell. Gia was his. She'd have to get over that stupid thought about tearing apart brothers because he didn't care at that moment.

The room broke into applause, and Dane turned back around to see a weepy Kent lift Bethany off the floor and kiss her as if he'd never kissed her before. The tears threatened again, but he wasn't going to have it. Dane batted them away before they had the chance to fall.

"I present to you, Mr. and Mrs. Kent and Bethany Black," the minister said as Kent and Bethany walked back down the aisle followed by their wedding party, who each took a moment to look directly at him.

Now he had to face the guests as he helped to empty the pews and escort the guests out of the church.

Chapter Twelve

Every guest had walked through the doors of the church when Russ grabbed Dane's arm.

"What the hell happened to you, baby?"

This was one of those moments when Russ should have gotten Dane's fist in his gut, but he refrained.

"Don't start. I don't need you to start with me."

Russ lifted his hands in surrender. "Just asking. Seriously, are you okay?"

"I'm fine. Don't ask again."

Russ gave him a nod and moved on.

Dane caught his reflection in the mirror at the back of the church. No doubt put there for people to look at them sorry selves after a wedding or a funeral to see how bad they looked.

"It was a beautiful ceremony, wasn't it?"

Her voice left his skin with goose bumps. Slowly, he turned to face her. Why not. It couldn't get any worse.

"It was nice, as far as weddings go," he said, noticing all of her makeup had nearly washed away from her tears.

"Do you think you and I can talk for a moment, away from everyone?"

Well, she'd seen him cry like a baby. Why not just kick him where it counts now? Certainly she wanted to have words with him. Now was as good a time as any.

Dane nodded for her to follow him to the cry room off to the side of the sanctuary—it seemed appropriate. He opened the door to the dark room that smelled of baby powder and something else, but he didn't want to think about that.

"What do you want to…"

Her hands went directly into his hair as she pressed her body against him and her lips to his.

Instinctively, he gathered her into his arms and let her take the kiss deeper as he held on for dear life.

There had to be some punishment for the sin she was diving into Gia thought as Dane's hands wandered up her back.

The kiss wasn't the plan. The moment wasn't supposed to happen like this, but she couldn't help herself. When their eyes had met, there was something pulling her to do what she was doing, and she didn't want to let go.

His hands slid from her back and to her waist before sliding over her rear and causing her to gasp.

"Sorry," he muttered as they kept their mouths joined.

He shouldn't be sorry. She was sorry. Sorry, she'd ever given him that load of bull that she didn't want to see him.

When solid thought stirred in her brain, she pulled back slightly so that she was still in his arms. "I didn't mean to do that," she said breathlessly as she pressed her forehead to his.

"I'm glad you did."

That made two of them. "I do not even remember what I wanted to talk to you about."

A grin formed on his swollen lips. "You're sure you had something to say?"

That was a moment for storming out, she thought, but she couldn't do it—didn't want to do it.

"I am sure."

"Your accent deepens when you're breathing heavy." His hands still gripped her tightly, and she took inventory of the beautiful sensations it gave her.

"So does yours," she said on a breath that should have slowed, but hadn't.

Finally, Dane stepped back and took a moment to collect himself by rubbing his hands over his face and hair. "I suppose they've noticed we disappeared together."

"I am sure. I am sorry. I do not know what came over me."

He turned, and his eyes burned into hers. "You don't know? I'll tell you," he said moving back to her. "It's that way that when we look at each other, our insides squeeze. When we talk, there's a giddy childishness to it. And damn it when we kiss…"

"There is a spark."

"Yeah, that's it," his breath was still airy and strained.

"But I meant what I said. I can not come between you and your brother. And you are leaving."

He nodded and kept his eyes still on hers. "I am leaving. And we can't do anything about this."

"Right."

Dane moved to her and placed his hands on her arms, rubbing them as if she were chilled, when certainly it was the opposite thanks to that kiss which still lingered on her lips.

"Today. We have today. We can live in the moment of that kiss and the knowledge that we feel something here. Something neither of us can quite ignore, but we're going to. Tomorrow we are going to go back to our lives, but we will have had this moment."

She hated it, but she knew he was right. This was what they had—this moment. "Okay. This moment. I will take it."

"You'll still be my date today?"

"There is no one I would rather be with."

He kissed her forehead, and the sweet gesture stirred her up inside more than the heated kiss.

"Let's get out there before they all burst in on us." He moved to open the door.

"I should fix my makeup. I am a sight."

He shook his head. "Bathroom is down the hall, but you look exquisite."

He gave her a wink as he left the room and the door shut behind him, leaving her alone with only the memory of him pressed against her.

Even now, she didn't know what she'd wanted to say to him. Perhaps she'd planned the kiss the entire time.

Gerald stood at the truck waiting for Dane. "I was sure you'd left me standing here looking like an idiot waiting for you. Where were you?"

"Just inside," Dane said as he opened the passenger door and climbed inside.

"With Gia?"

Why had he even asked if he knew. "Yes, I was talking to Gia."

Gerald nodded as he started the truck. "Russ thought so. He saw you go off with her. He decided to drive to the reception with Mom and Dad."

"Is he pissed?"

"No. Grow up. You can't come home and have everything about you."

"So I've been told."

Gerald stopped at the stop sign and checked traffic. "She's a hot number. I can't blame you for wanting her. Or Russ for wanting her. But he's cool."

Since they were having the conversation, Dane wasn't so sure Russ was cool about it, but he'd let it go. "We're just friends. We're going to attend the wedding together and tomorrow I'm leaving. Next time I'm home, she'll be in Italy. It could be a very long time before I see her again."

"The world is connected, and you of all people should know that," Gerald said as he picked up speed on the ramp to the highway. "Facebook, Twitter, Pinterest."

"I'm going to keep in touch with her on Pinterest?"

Gerald laughed. "Seriously, follow her boards and if you do make a thing of it, you'll know what to buy her."

That caused Dane to laugh. Who would have known his brother was so hip on keeping the ladies—especially since he didn't have one.

"I'd like just to keep her as a friend. Stalking her seems a little creepy."

Gerald shrugged. "It's invited stalking. Friend request her and see what happens."

He laughed again. There'd been too much arguing between Dane and his brothers. He needed to embrace these little moments and remember them when the other times got in the way.

~*~

The reception hall didn't even look the same. Gia took it in as she entered. Oh, she'd seen it as an empty space with only Lydia's imaginative words to describe it, but this had gone beyond her expectations.

The lights were low, and music played from the other side of the room, beyond the small dance floor. White lights were strung to give the room a subtle and beautiful glow.

Each table had a floral centerpiece with a floating candle in a vase of water. It was breathtaking.

"Your dance card is probably filled up." The voice behind her had her spinning around.

Russell Walker was handsome in his tuxedo and his perfectly groomed beard.

"Well, I do not know that it is full. I would be happy to…"

He took her hand and pressed a kiss to the back of it. "If Dane doesn't mind, I'd love a dance. But mostly, I'd like to apologize for the other day. Don't hold it against him. He likes you."

Her breath stuck in her lungs. What was she supposed to say to that?

"He's right you know," Dane's voice broke through the conversations around them. "I do like you. Don't hold his feelings against me."

Both of the men laughed, but she was surely too stunned to do so herself.

"I take it you two have mended your ways?" She pulled her hand back from Russell.

Dane rested his hand on his brother's shoulder. "We're brothers. That's how we take care of things."

She shook her head. "My brother never came at anyone of us to punch us."

"Of course not. You're not brothers. Trust me. That was nothing."

Gia felt as though she knew Glenda Walker well enough to assume she'd never let them attack each other on purpose. How was it brothers thought that hitting each other was the way to solve anything?

Russell gave Dane a solid slap on the back and walked away.

"So you guys talked?" Gia tucked her clutch under her arm.

"We did. I suppose you could call it that."

She narrowed her gaze on him. "You didn't hit him did you?"

"I want to say I did. I want to tell you that I physically won some challenge to get to dance with you tonight, but the truth is, we discussed it over fixing a gate. Manual labor does a body good."

"I will not come between brothers."

"You've said that. Besides, I think you and I know this is a very involved friendship."

"Right," she said clasping her hands in front of her. "No need to make it more complicated."

"Exactly. But if I were to friend you on Facebook, would you accept?"

Gia laughed easily and rested her hand on Dane's arm. "Of course, I would. You're quickly becoming one of my favorite friends."

Within the hour, the reception hall was filled with guests drinking and laughing. Bethany and Kent had danced their first dance, drank their champagne, and now were cutting into the beautiful cake.

Lydia had taken hold of Russell the moment Officer Smythe had walked into the room. Gia wondered what past they had. Lydia was appalled by the man, but he seemed to be wherever she was. Certainly there was a tale there.

Dane seemed to have been caught up with family most the night. Gia sipped champagne, tasted the cake, and now she thought she might sneak away and check in on her store around the corner. Only a few more weeks and she could start to move in.

She set her empty glass down on a tray and left the reception hall.

Opening her clutch, she pulled out the set of keys Pearl had made for her. She walked down the street, past Pearl's beautiful bridal boutique, and past the window display for the florist, who would be moving in soon as well.

When she made it to her door, she slipped in the key and pushed it open.

Dust from the drywall filled the air. There wasn't much to see, especially in the dark. She set her clutch down on a makeshift table and looked around.

The electrician had been working on the lights earlier that day, but the streetlight out front illuminated the room perfectly.

She could hear the music from the reception outside the back door. Everything about the building Pearl, Lydia, and Tyson bought was perfect, she thought.

"Are you running away from me?"

She spun to see Dane's body outlined in the doorway by the light on the street.

"You were busy, and I wanted to check in on the progress."

"You can't see anything," he said walking toward her. "It's dark."

Her breath caught as he neared. "There's a little light."

"Just enough to see your beautiful face," he said as he cupped her cheek with his hand.

"They will know you are missing."

"No one cares about me," he assured her, lifting his other hand to her face.

"I do."

Dane lowered a hand to her waist and the other to her hand. "Let's dance."

The soft music which cascaded down the hall gave them a rhythm. Dane pressed his cheek to hers, and they swayed back and forth in each other's arms.

She could feel his breath in her ear and her eyes closed as their bodies pressed together. After a few minutes, she wasn't sure she could even hear the music anymore. But the sound of her heartbeat echoed in her ears. All of this was only going to lead to more heartache.

When Dane quit moving back and forth, she looked up at him. His dark eyes locked onto hers. His hands moved into her hair, and he lowered his lips to hers and took the kiss she'd been wanting to give all night long.

Breath was fought for. Hands were controlled against the desire. Words—words were necessary now.

"Dane, what are we doing?" she asked, her eyes closed. Her head still spinning in the kiss.

"Living in the moment," his voice was a low growl as he took possession of her mouth once more.

Living in the moment wasn't necessarily something Gia did well. The last time she'd done such a thing, thrown caution to the wind, she'd ended up with a heart full of regret.

So why was she standing in the dark space of her new store holding on tightly to a man that was only going to leave in a few hours—because she couldn't fight the urge to be with him.

Dane stepped back. "What is that noise?"

All she could hear was her heartbeat pounding in her ears. Her mind took a moment to clear. "My cell phone. That is my mother's ringtone."

The rapid heartbeat that had deafened her now changed its pace. Gia moved quickly to where she'd set her clutch on the makeshift table. Dane followed, giving her the light from his phone to help her locate hers.

Panic had filled her body quickly. Dane watched her fumble to find the phone and then answer it.

He didn't know what time it was in Italy, but it had to be very early in the morning.

Gia spoke quickly in Italian. The volume of her voice had risen. His heart hitched when she covered hers with her hand.

"Mama," she said over and over.

Dane wanted to reach to her—touch her, but he refrained. He didn't understand a word she said, but when he saw the tear streak down her cheek, he reached for her hand.

She met his eyes with hers and in that moment his heart broke into a million pieces—though he didn't know why.

Gia finished her phone call with her mother and disconnected the call.

She began to speak to him, but it was all in Italian and just as fast as she'd spoken to her mother. When she looked up at him, the look of confusion must have shadowed his face, because she closed her eyes and let out a long sigh before looking at him again.

"I am sorry," she said softly and moved into his arms.

Gia sobbed against his chest as he held her. What could have hurt her so much?

"Sweetheart, is everything alright?"

"That was my mother. My sister-in-law has gone into labor."

At first, he wanted to laugh at the simple emotional silliness of the woman. Was she crying because a woman was having a baby? Then he remembered that the baby wasn't due until around Christmas. Gia was going home at Christmas to see the baby. It was only the end of September.

He gently peeled her back from him and looked down into her sad, wet eyes. "Gia, the baby?"

"We do not know anything yet. This baby is too early. Nearly two months too early."

"And they can't stop the labor?"

Gia shrugged. "My mother did not have all the details. She was scared, and that was why she called. My brother moved to Rome last year, and my mother cannot help out at a moment's notice."

"So maybe if they get her to the hospital they can stop the labor?"

She seemed to ease at that and moved in to rest her head against his chest again. "Perhaps." She swallowed one last sob. "My poor mother is so worked up, and I cannot be there to comfort her."

He smoothed his hand over her hair. "Maybe you should go home and call her back. Modern medicine is at work here. Even if the baby comes, I have no doubt that they will take care of him or her. Gia, everyone will be okay," he said, though he wasn't sure he was confident enough to believe it himself.

"I am glad you were here with me," she whispered as she stepped back from him. "This was not how I wanted our evening to end."

Now she'd put the dagger in his heart and threatened his manhood for turning her away.

"Your family needs you right now."

She nodded in agreement. "I will friend you on Facebook."

He chuckled at that. "I'd accept in a moment." Dane reached his hand to her cheek and held it there for a moment looking into her dark, sad eyes. "This isn't over, Gia. Our lives are tearing us into different directions for now. But I can't forget all of this."

She moved in and pressed her trembling lips to his. "I will never forget it either."

Gia quickly moved back and grabbed her purse, and they walked out into the dark street. He waited for her to lock the door before he walked her to her car and saw her off.

Her mother called again just as she'd unlocked the small car that gave her comfort. A moment later she sped off down the street leaving him alone—his heart aching for just one more night.

Chapter Thirteen

First snow had fallen in Columbus, Ohio on Halloween as the walking dead emerged to beg candy from strangers. Dane trudged through the wet accumulation from the bar he'd hold up at with co-workers blowing off steam after a recent downsize. He of course still had a job, only now he'd have more responsibility.

As he made his way to his apartment building, he passed a few ghouls and a princess, all of drinking age. He climbed the stairs, put his key in the lock, and opened the door to his unappealing home.

The only light was the one he left on over the stove. It was the only homey touch and reminded him of the light his mother would leave on for him when he'd come home as a teenager.

He threw his keys and phone on the table and walked to the refrigerator to look for a beer. There were two left. He pulled one out, looked at it, and put it back. More alcohol wasn't going to lift his mood any higher.

Dane walked to the couch, plopped down, and kicked off his wet shoes.

He tucked his hands under his head and leaned back—and Gia entered his mind.

She'd been there since they'd kissed goodbye. Not a day went by that he didn't think of her. It had been a month and she'd yet to accept his friend request on Facebook.

Russell had said he'd seen her packing up her store, but that he hadn't been in town much. It seemed Eric had landed quite a few horses to board, and they were all busy helping out.

He worried about her—dreamed about her.

Just as he'd decided to go to bed and put the day behind him, there was a knock at the door. He growled.

Maybe if he just ignored them, they'd go away, but they kept knocking.

Dane rose and walked to the door. "I don't have any candy," he grunted.

"Dane, open the door. I have to pee."

He pulled open the door to see Piper, his next door neighbor, dressed as a fairy, hopping up and down. "You can't pee at your place?"

"I forgot my key again," she said pushing past him and running down the hall to the bathroom.

He chuckled as he shut the door. She was all of twenty-two-years-old, but she seemed to like hanging around with him. Why he had no idea. He certainly wasn't any fun. She tended to lock herself out of her apartment at least once a week too. He figured that was a game she played with her mother, though. He'd heard the story. Piper's mother had divorced husband number three when Piper was a senior in high school. They packed up the mini-van and moved. Now her mother had shacked up with another man, as Piper had put it, but she still paid the rent. Dane figured that by locking herself out of the apartment once a week, it made her mother take note of her.

A moment later Piper skipped out of the bathroom. "Did you go out tonight?" she asked as she fell onto his couch and kicked her feet up on the coffee table.

"Had drinks with some co-workers. Did you call your mom?"

"She's not answering," she said through gritted teeth. "I've texted, called, Facebooked, and even called her *man*. Hell if I know where she is."

Dane pinched the bridge of his nose. "Should we call the superintendent?"

Piper shook her head. "He threatened to kick us out if I made him open the door one more time."

"Can he do that?"

She shrugged. "I didn't ask again. He freaks me out."

He freaked Dane out too. "Maybe you should leave a key here," he offered, but he knew that would end the game she was playing.

He looked at his watch. "It's late, and I have to work tomorrow."

"I can just wait for her. I won't be a bother to you."

He looked at her all comfy on his couch as if she belonged there in her fairy costume.

"Leave me a note or something when you leave, okay?" God, he sounded like his mother.

Piper smiled. "You're a solid friend, Dane."

He gave her a nod and headed to his bedroom. Sleep was calling.

~*~

Gia stared at her phone. Where had the time gone the past month? She saw the profile image of Dane and Ben on a set of dirt bikes outside Eric's barn on Dane's Facebook page. They'd talked about keeping in touch, but they had clearly not kept to that promise.

She looked at her friend requests, and he'd sent her one the day after the wedding. This was the first time she'd looked. He must have thought she was ignoring him completely.

There was so much to share with him, but as he hadn't called or texted, maybe he wasn't interested.

She accepted the friend request, looked at the time, and decided she'd call him anyway.

It was only ten o'clock. Surely she wouldn't be bothering him.

The phone had rung three times before she heard the sound of it being answered and tousled around.

"Hello? Hello? Did I lose you? I dropped the damn phone," a woman said and laughed. "Might have had a few too many drinks," she laughed again.

"Hello?" Gia said. "Dane?"

The woman laughed even harder. "No. It's Piper. Who's this?"

Gia felt the will to continue the conversation slip from her as she eased back in her oversized chair and let the pain of the moment envelop her.

"This is Gia. I was just calling to say hello to Dane, but..."

"Where are you from? You have the most awesome accent."

Gia bit down hard. Who was this tart? "I am from Italy."

"Oh, that is so cool. I've never been anywhere. I mean I've moved around, but nowhere as cool as Italy. Say something in Italian."

"I am sorry. I seem to have bothered you. Perhaps I have the wrong number."

"Nah," Piper said. "You're not bothering me. Dane's phone rang. I answered. I got nothing else to do."

"So I did reach Dane's phone?"

"Yup."

"He must be busy. Can you just tell him I called?"

"Oh, hold on. He's in bed. I'll get him."

Her words ripped right through Gia. "No. No. Oh, no, do not get him. This is not important. I will talk to him some other time." Like never, she thought.

"Whatever. It was cool to talk to you. Later." And the line went dead.

There was no way to fight the release of angry tears. What had she thought? As if he'd have meant anything he said. He was a man and men were stupid animals. She'd had proof of that for years. It was a man that had her leaving her home and living thousands of miles away, after all. To hell with Dane Walker.

She looked at the app on her phone and went to click *unfriend*, then stopped. No. She wouldn't unfriend him, not yet. She wanted to see if he even noticed that she'd reached out. He deserved some of this pain too.

~*~

Dane scrubbed his hands over his face as he stumbled his way to the coffee pot. Any other year, a Halloween on a Friday would have been welcomed. But that specific Friday had been horrible for so many others.

The downsizing of his office had hit many of them as a surprise. It shouldn't have, though. They'd all seen it coming. Perhaps the true surprise was that he still had a job.

Drinking away the sorrows of those who had been let go might have been a mistake, however. He'd been informed, before the release of nearly half of his co-workers, that he'd be expected in the office for the next few weeks on Saturdays.

As he took the coffee pot and filled it with water, he yawned. He continued pouring the water into the maker, measuring out the coffee grounds, and then he waited.

He closed his eyes as he leaned up against the counter. What he wouldn't give to…

He heard a noise that took him off guard.

Dane moved around the corner and looked in the living room. There was Piper, snoring softly on his couch.

Obviously, her mother hadn't come to her rescue. He'd figured that was coming.

Once his coffee had brewed, he poured himself a cup and then one for Piper.

He walked it out to the couch and set the cup on the table before giving her a gentle shake.

"Hey, I made you some coffee."

Piper stirred, and he shook her again.

"Piper, wake up."

She stirred, yawned, and her eyes opened slightly.

Dane sipped his coffee and watched her. It saddened him to see this young woman sleeping on his couch simply because she was seeking someone's attention. Perhaps he should be honored that she chose his couch. The sad thought crossed his mind. She probably slept on the couches of many other men who weren't there for her as a person, but for their own selfish need.

Piper wiped at her eyes. "Why are you up?" Her voice was full of gravel. "It's Saturday."

"I have to go to work. Have you talked to your mom?"

She looked around for her phone, finding it tucked in the cushion of the couch. She opened her eyes further and blinked them a few times as she focused on the screen. "Looks like she came by and put it above your door."

Dane walked to the door, opened it, and felt above the frame for the key. Just as promised, there it was.

"Why don't you go home and get yourself together. I have to go into the office. We could grab a bagel and stop by a hardware store and get a copy of this key made," he said holding it in his hand.

"I kinda drank all my money last night," she said scooping her hair back.

Dane shook his head. "I'll buy you a bagel. But you have to promise me you'll lay low this week. Go to work and come home. You're better than locking yourself out of your apartment."

She didn't argue with him, which told him she knew he was right. "I'll change and put my hair up," she said standing and stretching her arms over her head.

"I have to get ready too."

She walked toward the door. "It must suck to have to work on Saturday."

Dane shrugged. "It's not forever."

She gave him a wink and disappeared as she closed the door behind her.

An hour later they were in his office, a tray of coffee and a bag of bagels sat on his desk between them.

As he waited for his computer to start up, he picked up his coffee and sat back in his chair. Piper picked up her coffee and sat on Dane's desk.

"You're stuck in this place every day?" she asked as she lifted her cup to her lips and blew through the hole in the lid.

Dane shrugged. "It's how it has to be. Gotta have a job to pay the bills."

She nodded. "I guess I'll take my bagel and coffee and head out of here."

"You don't want to hang out in this place?" he joked as she stood and picked up her bag which contained her onion bagel with cream cheese.

"You're not keen on hanging here, huh?"

Piper laughed. "You're cute and all. But not enough my type to want to hang around here."

"That hurts."

Piper walked around the desk and pressed a kiss to his cheek. "You'll survive," she said as she backed away and headed for the door. "By the way, who's the Italian?"

"What?"

"She called your phone last night after you went to bed. She sounds sexy."

Dane stood quickly and pulled his phone from his pocket. "You didn't tell me she called?"

"Didn't know it was a big deal. I'll catch ya later. Thanks for letting me stay last night." She gave him a slight wave and headed out.

Dane scrolled through his phone and saw that the call had come in at nearly ten o'clock last night.

Things had gotten in the way the past month, and he hadn't talked to her at all. Why had she called last night, and what had Piper said to her?

As soon as the screen on his computer popped up with a picture of a beach, he clicked on the Facebook logo and saw his timeline appear. She'd accepted his friendship, finally.

Now all he had to do was reach out to her.

Just as he began a message to her, Ralph, his boss, walked in the door and dropped a stack of papers on his desk. "New York is a week away. We have a lot of work to do before then, and now it's only you, me, and Paul going. We're meeting in the conference room in five." With that, he headed back out of the office.

Dane closed off the window on his computer and picked up the papers Ralph had dropped on his desk. Once again, work was going to get in the way of his life.

Chapter Fourteen

November in New York City was downright miserable in the weather department, but it was too glorious a city to make Gia worry about the cold. She cinched up her coat, keeping her purse securely tucked underneath.

She walked out onto the street, away from the convention center where she'd been viewing new products from vendors all over the world.

Once in a while, she'd purchase items that hadn't come from Lucca. Now that her store was bigger, she could carry items from all over Italy, and not just Tuscany.

Gia watched the people that exited the convention center. Her hotel was to the right, but sometimes it was much more fun to go the opposite direction. She decided to follow the small group which had exited the center a few minutes before her. She'd heard them say something about sushi, and well, that just sounded good now.

Three men walked toward her, their phones in their hands, and none of them was talking to one another. She realized they didn't see her at all. They were focused on something and heading right to the center she'd just left.

She wondered at what point one of them was going to look up before they walked right into her.

As if they knew there was traffic in their way, they formed a straight line and headed toward the door of the center.

The man who had landed at the end of their little line looked up briefly as if to look ahead, and then his head dipped back down to his phone.

Gia spun to watch the man head for the door before she called after him. "Dane?"

The man stopped, as well as the two other men in front of him.

When his eyes shifted from his phone and up to her, they went wide. A smile was instant to his lips, and he moved to her quickly, pulling her into his arms.

She rocked on her heels, trying to keep her balance, and instinctively wrapping her arms around his neck.

"I had no idea you were here," he said in her ear before he pulled back and looked at her. "What are you doing here?"

"Buyers' convention. And you?"

"Software writer seminar. Nothing as exciting." His eyes were still wide. The thought that he was genuinely happy to see her thrilled her, but she couldn't forget the voice on the end of his phone the night she called. Suddenly she could feel the cold that blew through the city as it penetrated her jacket.

"It was nice to see you," she said hoping that the chill in her voice matched the air that blew his hair into a mess that she fought the urge to fix with her fingers. Gia turned to walk away.

"Wait a minute." He took her arm and turned her back to him. "You're not walking off are you? I thought we were better friends than that."

His idea of friendship was much different than hers, she decided. But the look of desperation in his eyes had her standing there contemplating it.

He turned toward the men who waited for him. "Go on in. I'll be a few more minutes."

She wondered what was going to take him so long. She had no intent to stand there in the cold and discuss what friendship meant. They'd obviously both failed at it.

"You should go. You have important work to do," she demanded, but his hand was still on her arm, and she didn't shake him lose.

"I've missed you," he said, and his voice had gone soft. "I really have missed you."

This was no time for her to go weak, and she could feel her knees wanting give.

"I doubt that very much, Mr. Walker. It has been well over a month since we have spoken. Obviously, whatever we thought we had, it was not much."

"We've both been busy. How is your brother's baby?"

The air in her lungs froze when she sucked in a breath to keep the tears from stinging her eyes when he asked about her family. The compassion in his eyes was real, that much she could see.

"They stopped the contractions that night. She has been on bed rest since. My mother is staying with them to take care of the other children. I assume that any day they will call with news that the baby is here." A smile crept across her lips. She couldn't help but smile when she thought of her family and the baby that she would meet at Christmas.

His hand slipped from her arm to her hand. "I'm glad everything is okay. I should have called after the wedding. I should have…"

Gia lifted a finger to his lips. "We are both busy people." She lowered her hand. "We got caught up in the moment."

Her words hurt him. She could see it flash over his face.

"Caught up in the moment?" His voice shook when he spoke.

"Obviously, that is what happened. People do not just forget about one another if it meant something."

She saw the vein in his neck throb as he tightened his jaw. "I don't know what you think that was then. It was more than just a moment to me."

Gia couldn't bite her tongue anymore. "I am very sure Piper would not think of it that way."

He actually staggered back, and that gave her a moment of satisfaction. He deserved to hurt for that.

"She told me you called."

"Oh, I see that her secretarial skills are intact. She sounded very young, Dane. Is that so you can groom her?"

His lips were tights and his eyes narrowed. "Is that what you think? You think I have something with Piper?"

"Really, what else would I think when a woman answers your phone at ten o'clock at night and tells me you are in bed."

He looked away. Whatever she was thinking might have been true. Why else would he be so irritated?

"You are a piece of work. You know that?" He shoved his hands into his coat pockets. "Piper is my neighbor who locked herself out of her apartment. She was waiting for her mother to bring the key. I'm not involved with her or anyone for that fact. I've been a little preoccupied in that department with you in my head. But when I got back to Ohio they laid off half of my team, and I've been busting my ass for…" He let out a long breath, and it carried on the air in a cold cloud. "This is worthless. I didn't call you either. I didn't reach out to check on your family. I can see why you're so standoffish."

He looked back toward the building where the men had gone inside as he'd told them to do. "I guess this is goodbye," he said.

Gia could feel the tremble in her lips as he turned from her and began to walk toward the doors. This wasn't what she wanted. She'd thought too much of him to watch him walk away.

"Dane," she called after him and watched him turn around.

Their eyes met, locked—connected. She took a breath and ran toward him. His hands came around her waist and hers around his neck. Their lips, cold to the touch, warmed as they pressed them against one another's. Breath mixed with the air around them and each of them panted for it as they deepened the kiss that they both needed so desperately.

"I do not want this to end like that," she said laying her head on his chest.

He stroked a hand down her hair. "I don't either. I haven't been able to concentrate very much. You've been on my mind."

Gia chuckled. "This should be a sign, right? We are both here at the same time."

"I got here today," he said pulling back to look down at her. "I'm here for three more days."

She felt the crushing pain in her chest of regret. "I leave bright and early in the morning."

He nodded. "Of course. This seems to be how it works for us."

The grief of the moment was horrible, but it was true. She already knew that when he was in Georgia again, for Christmas, she'd be in Italy. Perhaps this love affair they were trying to have wasn't realistic at all. But at least they'd seemed to have mended their friendship.

"How long are your meetings today?"

"They go until six and then we're meeting with the corporate head for dinner."

She nodded. "Maybe we could keep in touch better from now on. I will make a better effort."

"Me too," he promised as he placed his cold hand on her cheek. "I wish we had more time."

"That does not seem to be in the stars for us," she admitted, her voice dripping in the sorrow that coursed through her body.

Dane lowered his lips to hers one last time, and she let the kiss warm her, hoping to hold on to its memory forever.

As he pulled away, he kept his eyes locked with hers until he turned and disappeared into the building.

She could feel the tears fighting to surface. Perhaps the cold kept them at bay. She watched him walk away from her, as she'd done to him the last time they'd been together.

Gia decided to head back to her hotel. She no longer wished to explore the city. The comfort of a warm shower and a bottle of wine would be more her style. She needed to wallow in her self-pity for the night.

She mixed with the crowd that huddled at the stoplight waiting to cross. The noise of the city burned her ears. Cars, horns and the voices of people around her scratched at her until she wanted to scream.

As the light turned, and the crowd moved across the street, she heard her name in the air.

Certainly she was hearing things. No one but Dane knew she was there.

As she stepped up on the curb on the other side, she heard it again. With the crowd bumping into her as she stopped, she turned to see Dane running her way from the convention center.

She moved to the corner where a new crowd had formed to wait to cross as the traffic cut off the access to the street.

He ran to the corner and stopped in a crowd on the other side.

Their eyes locked with each other's, and if his heart beat nearly as fast as hers, she was sure it would drown out the noises around them.

It had seemed like forever before the lights changed and the crowds blended in the middle of the street, which was where she found him.

He picked her up, cradled in his arms, and carried her to the sidewalk where he gently set her down and kissed her as people passed by and bumped into them.

"I can't go back in there. I want to be with you."

"Dane…"

"No. Nothing else is as important." He kissed her again. "Let's go back to your hotel. Gia, I want to be with you." Pressing his forehead to hers and cupping her face in his hands he whispered, "God, I want to be with you."

She should argue. This meant his job, and she knew it. But she had to be with him and be wrapped in his arms.

With a nod, she took hold of his hand and dragged him down the street toward her hotel. Nothing could get them there any faster than the sheer will to want to make love to the man before they were separated again.

Chapter Fifteen

Dane wasn't sure he'd ever run so quickly in his life. Of course, he'd never wanted anything so much in life.

Gia pulled him by the hand through the door of the hotel and to the elevator. She wrapped her arms around him as they waited for the doors to open, and when they did, she pulled him inside. Unfortunately, an older couple joined them, which was a shame.

She looked up at him, her lips moist from her tongue's trail over them.

He fisted his hands to his side. He would die if the elevator got stuck.

Four more floors to go, he noted as the numbers rose, and then stopped. The couple exited, and before the doors were closed, Gia moved into his arms and took possession of his mouth drowning him with the passion she promised.

The door opened, and they stumbled out into the hall, their lips still locked to one another as they fumbled against walls and doorways until they reached her door.

She pulled her key card from her purse and turned to unlock the door. Dane pushed her hair from her neck and pressed a kiss to her soft skin. He felt her body ease back against him.

Gia pushed open the door, and they rode the wave of passion inside, kicking it closed behind them.

~*~

Gia could hear the city below them and see the glow of its lights from the window. It was nearly one in the morning, and she was afraid to move, almost afraid to breathe.

Dane's arms were wrapped around her, and his breath was soft on her neck.

Their minutes together ticked away as she absorbed every moment they'd spent in that bed wrapped around each other.

She closed her eyes and breathed in his scent. She'd never forget it.

He'd loved her as no man ever had. Not that she'd had many lovers, but Dane—she let out a breath—he was attentive.

Dane stirred behind her, and his arms tightened around her. His lips moved against her neck, and she let out a sigh.

"What time is it?" His voice was soft.

"One o'clock."

He hummed his understanding against her skin. "I'm hungry."

"We could order up food."

"I'd like that."

Gia rolled in his arms to face him. "What should we eat."

His eyes were still dark with sleep as he smiled. "I could nibble on you the rest the night."

"I am having second thoughts all of this," her voice shook with the nerves that had taken her stomach and twisted it as she looked into his eyes.

"Don't." He nipped her nose with a kiss. "This was the most amazing night of my life."

That had her chuckling. "Most amazing night? That is quite a compliment."

Dane reached his fingers into her hair. "It should be." He moved so that she rolled onto her back and his body hovered over hers. "Maybe I'm not so hungry right now."

"We only have a few more hours before I have to catch my flight."

The disappointment flashed on his shadowed face in the dark. "Then I don't want to waste a moment of it not kissing you."

His lips met hers and the rest of their night was spent as the first of it had been—making passionate love. But it stuck in her head that she'd be leaving him soon. There were no promises between them, only the moment. She'd have to take these memories with her because that would be all she'd have left.

~*~

Gia had flown all over the world. She'd had bumpy flights and hard landings but never had a flight been so painful as the one she was now taking.

Dane's touch still lingered on her skin and his kiss was still fresh on her lips. Life pulled them apart again, and she just wasn't sure she could get used to it.

They had talked about seeing each other at Thanksgiving. It was only a few weeks away. The thought had to carry her until then because she already missed him.

But Thanksgiving was only a few days long. What would happen after that? They'd already discussed the fact that she'd be in Italy for Christmas. And if he kept his job, after having run out yesterday, he wouldn't be able to get away to visit. Likewise, with the new store and her trip to Italy, she couldn't expect to leave anytime soon either.

They'd agreed to face-time and text. Maybe something would come of the amazing night she'd had with the man who had occupied her mind for months. Or maybe it would be a glorious memory she took with her into the rest of her life.

The moment she landed, she texted Dane to let him know she was on the ground. She couldn't help the disappointment that filled her when she got home, and he still hadn't responded. That wasn't fair to him she thought as she set her suitcase in the living room and walked about to make sure everything was as she'd left it.

As she walked from room to room, she thought about what he might be going through. He had to be fighting for his job. What if a night with her cost him that?

He didn't seem to like the job, but she didn't want to be his reason for losing it.

Her phone rang, and she hurried back to the living room where her purse sat with her luggage. The racing of her heart had her gulping in a breath of air, but only disappointment followed when she looked at the caller ID.

"*Pronto*," she said waiting for her mother to talk on the other end.

Her mother was in tears again, but this time, the sound of her voice was much different. The news that she was an aunt to a new niece filled the void in her heart that had been there the moment she kissed Dane goodbye.

Luckily everything had gone smoothly, and her niece was healthy after the scare last month. As soon as her mother hung up the phone, she was instantly homesick.

Soon, she'd be home soon.

Gia went on to unpack and regain some normalcy to her evening. When her brother called, she wept at hearing about the baby. He sent her pictures, and she fell in love.

She caught up with Sunshine, who had stepped in and ran the store while she was in New York. Nothing much had happened while she was gone, but that was just how she wanted it.

It wasn't long before the trip to New York, and the night with no sleep, caught up with her. She sent another text to Dane before went to bed and quickly drifted to sleep thinking of him.

~*~

Dane listened to his co-worker recap the information from the day before. They'd covered for him, telling their boss that he'd gotten sick, thought Dane never told them why he'd run off.

Those were good friends. Those that didn't ask too many questions and still covered a guy's ass. He owed it to them to get back on track.

He'd seen Gia's texts come through, but he didn't just want to text her back. He wanted to hear her voice or see her face. He wanted to touch her skin and feel her in his arms—that's what he wanted.

The day continued to be nonstop. Meeting after meeting. The boss flew in, and they had lunch. More proving himself worthy, and then dinner in Time Square.

By the time he got back to his hotel room, it was after midnight. There was no way he'd call or text her now. Well, maybe he'd shoot her off a text.

Can't stop thinking about you, he typed into his phone and then laid it on his chest as he closed his eyes for a moment, hoping she'd text back.

The pounding at his door had him sitting up straight. His phone flew to the floor. He squinted his eyes from the sun—*the sun!* Oh, dear God! He'd fallen asleep waiting for her text.

Dane pulled open his door to find his boss on the other side.

"We were supposed to meet for breakfast," he said very sternly.

"Right. We were. I overslept. I…"

"You'll need to be at the convention center in thirty-five minutes," he warned as he walked away.

Dane nodded and quickly shut the door. He looked down at his phone. The message he had tried to send to Gia still sat there, *unable to send*. He let out a grunt. Just as he tried to resend the text his phone shut down. He hadn't charged it, and now it was dead.

Two days ago he had the woman of his dreams in his arms while he held her in her bed. Now he was scrambling not to lose everything he'd worked so hard for.

Seriously, New York could kiss his ass.

Chapter Sixteen

Sunshine had offered to help Gia organize the store so they could begin to decorate for Christmas. It was forgivable to do so in the retail business. In fact, Gia thought she should have had a Christmas tree up before Halloween. As it was, here they were, putting up the tree only a day before Thanksgiving.

Glenda had invited her over for Thanksgiving dinner. Though the offer was very generous, it surprised her a bit. She wondered what she knew about her and Dane.

Gia had only spoken to him a few times since they'd last seen each other. Even the thought of that night made her skin warm.

He hadn't even mentioned Thanksgiving. Perhaps inviting her over was Glenda's way of accepting their relationship—or fling. Gia wasn't sure what to think of it. They were both grown adults with other passions. Perhaps *fling* was a better term.

"I love the ornaments you ordered from Venice. These are great," Sunshine admired the hand blown glass ornaments as she placed them on the tree.

"It is a little shop off the plaza near Saint Mark's. There are so many cute stores there. Now that I have more room here, I can enjoy shopping there even more."

Sunshine laughed. "Where else?"

"Well, there is a Venetian island, Burano, where they make lace. It will be the next item I bring in."

"Oh, lace! My mother loves lace."

"She will be very happy then. It is a beautiful place."

The door opened, and Lydia walked in with an enormous box in her arms. Officer Smythe walked in behind her carrying two large boxes as well.

"What is all of this?" Gia asked.

Lydia set the box on the counter. "They were delivered to the reception hall yesterday." She shifted a glance to Officer Smythe and snarled. "Put them down."

He grinned and set them on the floor next to the counter.

Gia walked over to them and looked at the boxes. "I was not expecting anything."

Lydia shrugged. "I don't know." She looked at Smythe again. "You can go now. You've done your duty of chivalry."

Any other man might have stormed out, but Officer Smythe smiled and walked out of the store.

"Ass," Lydia said under her breath.

"How did you get him to help you?" Gia amused herself.

"Suddenly he thinks he needs to check the area every few days. He's in my way, just like he always is. I hate that man, and he knows it. So why come around?"

Sunshine walked over to them. "He likes you. It's obvious."

"He's a womanizer and just a country idiot. He makes my skin crawl."

Gia wasn't sure about that, but the feud between Lydia and Officer Smythe was something of near legend.

Lydia stepped back from the counter. "Open them. Now you have me curious. They came from Italy."

Gia was wracking her brain trying to figure out what it was that she'd ordered when the door to her store opened.

She looked at the man that walked in and the breath from her lungs whooshed out leaving her dizzy.

"*Buongiorno*, Gia."

She could see Lydia swoon from the corner of her eye, but there was no need for it, Gia thought. This man, who stood before them, made her skin crawl just as Officer Smythe did to Lydia.

"Marco."

"No hug?" His accent was thick with the sound of home.

"What are you doing here?"

He smiled and unbuttoned his coat. "I came to visit you."

"You never called."

"That would have ruined the surprise." He looked at the other women who stood on each side of her. "Are you going to introduce me to your friends?" His English was much better than she'd remembered.

Gia thought about it for a moment and did as he asked. "This is Sunshine, she helps out once in a while, but works at the bridal shop next door."

Marco took Sunshine's hand and kissed it. "Pleased to meet you."

"Likewise," Sunshine said and her Southern drawl deepened.

"This is Lydia," Gia turned toward the other woman whose eyes had gone wide. "She owns the building."

"I like a woman who seeks adventure such as owning property," he said taking her hand and kissing it as well.

"I own a lot of properties in town. And you're right, it is an adventure," she nearly giggled when she spoke. "Sunshine and I should let you two catch up."

That was the last thing Gia wanted them to do, but Sunshine grabbed her coat, and they both scurried out of her store and headed toward Pearl's bridal store.

Now she was alone with Marco, with nothing but Italy surrounding them. He moved in and took her hands.

"I have missed you, Bella."

"Do not call me that," she argued. "I am not yours to speak to like that."

The grin on his lips, those perfect lips, never shifted. And those eyes, those dark chocolate eyes, pierced right into her.

"You will always be mine. We are destined."

Why couldn't she pull her hands from his? Marco leaned in to kiss her cheek. She shifted to pull away, but instead she moved the wrong direction, and her lips were caught under his.

When she did manage a step back, he was grinning wider. "You should open your packages."

"I did not order anything."

"My aunt sends them. She hopes for a consignment from you."

Gia bit down. "That is very thoughtful. I will speak to her when I go home. Please let her now."

He moved toward her again and she backed herself behind the counter. "Why do you stay here? I offered you the world at your fingertips. You would not need to work like this."

"I did not want your world. I am not a woman to stay home while her man is away—or with someone else," she added that last jab into the message she was hoping to convey.

"I thought you were raised to forgive."

She lifted her chin. "Forgive, maybe. Forget, never."

He grinned again and she fisted her hands at her side. She was weak when it came to this man. She didn't want to be weak any longer.

As if she'd willed it, her cell phone rang, and she picked it up quickly. "*Prego,*" her Italian took over instinctively.

"Gia?"

"Dane," his name slipped from her lips with a sigh.

"Did I catch you at a bad time?"

"No. I just am finishing up with a customer. Can you hold for a moment?"

She shifted the phone so that her hand cupped it and Dane could not hear her.

"It is time for you to go."

He shook his head. "Dinner. Tonight. I will pick you up."

She took a breath to protest, but he winked at her and walked out of the store. Her heart raced uncomfortably, fueled by anger.

Trying to calm herself enough to steady her voice, she lifted the phone to her ear. "Hello."

"I love to hear your voice," Dane said. "I wanted to apologize. I haven't had much time to call."

"I understand," her voice shook, and she fought to control it. "You're busy."

"They did a second round of layoffs today."

"Did you lose your job?"

He chuckled. "Amazingly enough, no. Somehow I scathed through New York without losing my job."

She wanted to laugh with him, but it ached to think of New York. "Are you headed home now? I mean, are you in route here?" One more day and she could see him again. They could hold one another. She could feel safe and secure in his arms.

"That's why I'm calling." He let out a long breath. "I can't be there."

Her hand began to shake and tears threatened. "I do not know what to say. I was looking forward to you coming."

"Yeah, so was I. I sure didn't mean for this to happen, Gia. But I wanted you to know I wasn't avoiding you."

Certainly she didn't think that. She had, however, begun to think they were just star-crossed lovers who were never going to have a chance.

"Gia, maybe we could plan a weekend. You could come up."

"Not during this time of year," she said sadly. "I am busy right up till Christmas."

"I hadn't thought of that. But at Christmas…"

"I will be in Italy."

She heard the groan through the phone. "That's right." There was a moment of silence. "How do people do this?"

"Do what?"

"Have long distance relationships."

Her heart fluttered in her chest. "Relationship? Is that what we have?"

"Yeah," the word came quickly and with certainty. "Gia, I don't do what we did casually."

She was smiling. "Neither do I."

"I have to get some work done, but I'll call you later."

They said goodbye, and she disconnected the call. They were in a relationship. She drew in the thought like a breath of fresh air. Suddenly the surprises of the day and the disappointments were washed away. Dane Walker still wanted her and time would be theirs—eventually.

Chapter Seventeen

After Dane had called, Gia hadn't thought much more about what had happened earlier that day, until Marco walked through her door ten minutes before closing.

She bit back the anger. She was in a relationship with Dane Walker, and if she remembered correctly, Marco was married.

"*Buona Sera*, Gia."

She'd refrain from the properness. "Marco."

"Are you ready for dinner?"

She fisted her hands on her hips. "I do not think dinner with you is a good idea."

He winked. "Did you have something better in mind?"

This was why the man made her so irritated. "No."

"All I ask is dinner."

"And all I asked was for your loyalty."

He nodded slowly. "I deserve that."

"You do, and so much more."

Marco moved to stand in front of her. "I was wrong. I apologize."

"And I no longer care. Your apology means nothing."

He reached for her hand on her hip and held it in his. "You can hate me forever, but I am here right now, and I would like two old friends to have dinner together. That is all."

"Where is your wife?" She had to ask, as much for the knowledge as for the jab at him.

Marco released her hand and paced a small circle. "You do not keep up with your family as much as I thought you might."

"My family does not believe in gossip."

"True." He stood in front of her and rocked back on his heels. "My wife left me."

"Wise woman."

"Oh, now, Gia. I am not so bad."

"Then tell me, why did she leave you."

His lips puckered. "It seems I had a woman on my mind too often. A woman I had scorned and it ate at me."

Now her heart raced at his words. She'd left Italy to get away from this man who had stolen her heart and stomped on it. Why did he now stand in front of her feeding her these emotional lines? And why was she buying them and feeling for him?

He took her hands in his again. "I never stopped loving you, Gia. No woman has ever come close to you."

"I was not enough then."

"I was foolish."

"You are an idiot."

He chuckled. "I am." He lifted a hand to her cheek. "Let me kiss you."

She found herself leaning in to let him do just that, but then pulled away and turned from him. "I cannot do this. I am seeing someone."

Marco tucked his hands into his pockets. "Are you now? Who might that be?"

"Dane Walker."

"And where is Mr. Walker? I would like to meet him and give my approval."

"Your approval?" Now the furry was back, and it was aimed at Marco, just as it should have been the moment he walked through the door. "I do not need your approval. I never needed your approval. I despise what you brought to me. As far as I am concerned, you wasted a lot of time coming to America. How could you ever have thought that I would want to be with you again?"

Marco nodded. "You are right. I should have thought better of it." He moved to her, but she stood steady. "I miss you, Gia. My heart is yours, and if you should ever see it in your heart to forgive me, I will be there for you."

He turned and walked back through the store. "You have a fine place here, Gia. Your father would be proud of what you have done."

She waited until he'd closed the door and was on the other side before she let the tears that had built up fall. Marco was her first love, and he betrayed her. It was bad enough she left her family and her home to start all over again. Now she'd fallen for a man who she couldn't even be with, and her heart ached just to be in his arms.

Perhaps love wasn't for Gia. Perhaps she was meant always to be alone.

She hurried to the door and locked it. Tonight she would stay late and finish all the decorating. Tomorrow she would have dinner with Dane's family. Then she would discuss having Sunshine cover the store for her for a few weeks. Christmas suddenly seemed so far away, and she needed the strength of her family now. She needed to hold her niece and cuddle her other niece and nephew. Her sister needed her blessing, in person, to marry the man she loved and she needed her mother's cooking and her father's wise words.

It all hurt so much now, after seeing Marco, and remembering his touch and his betrayal. If only Dane were closer, maybe none of this would matter. But it did, and she needed to mend her heart and soon.

~*~

Gia spent her evening making cookies to take to the dinner. Glenda said that she and Susan had the main meal prepared. Pearl and Audrey were in charge of bread. Bethany was bringing a salad. The men were all in charge of simple things, as Glenda hadn't wanted them in her kitchen, or so she had joked when she'd invited Gia.

Making the cookies was supposed to be her part in sharing her traditional recipes, but it became the therapy she desperately needed to combat her day.

Marco hadn't returned to the store or stop by her house. She was grateful for that. A call to her mother, early in Lucca, completed the mend that she needed. When she told her mother that she was planning an earlier trip, her mother cried. They all needed each other.

Dinner at the Walker's was scheduled for two in the afternoon. When Gia arrived, all of the men and Pearl were planted in front of the TV watching a football game. Susan took the plate of cookies from her and walked her back to the kitchen, her arm wrapped around her shoulder, where Glenda enveloped her in a hug.

"I'm so glad you're joining us today. This is very special."

"Thank you for inviting me. It was very thoughtful."

Glenda patted her face, much as her mother would too. "I'm enjoying everyone here. I wish Dane could be here, but having Susan, Kent, and Tyson here, it almost makes up for it." She leaned in closer. "You know what happens when all the children get married? They have babies," she whispered.

Susan laughed loudly. "Becoming anxious?"

Glenda grinned as she went back to the task of tossing a salad. "A woman with children always looks forward to grandchildren. And my sons are pushing it. Some of them are inching out of child rearing days," she said looking directly at Susan. "You're now my only hope."

There was a blush on Susan's cheeks. "I'll see what I can do."

Gia missed her mother even more as she watched Glenda and Susan banter. Tears stung her eyes and she batted them away, but not before Bethany noticed.

"Are you okay?"

"I am missing my family lately. My niece was born and," she sucked in a breath, "I am just a bit homesick."

"Then you're in for a treat," Bethany moved toward her. "I was helping out at the reception hall the other day when a man delivered some items for you. He said you were old friends."

Gia felt a tightening in her chest as she watched Bethany's eyes widen.

"I invited him to dinner. I wanted to surprise you."

There was a knot in Gia's stomach that nearly had her doubled over. "He is here?"

"Not yet, but he will be soon." She was smiling so wildly that Gia didn't want to let her down, but she'd much rather go home now.

A moment later the doorbell rang and then she heard his voice. He'd double-crossed her. Marco knew he'd see her again.

"*Buona Sera*," his voice boomed in the room.

Bethany moved to him, nearly floating above the floor. "Marco, I'm so glad you could make it."

He took her hand and kissed it, almost as if he'd walked out of a movie. "*Grazie*. It is so nice to know Gia has such good friends in America."

She felt her skin grow cold as he warmed up to the women in the kitchen, introducing himself as if he were some debutant.

He then moved to her and wrapped his arm around her waist. "Gia and I go way back. Childhood."

Glenda shifted a glance her way. "Is that so?"

It took everything Gia had to put a smile on her lips. "Yes, we have been *friends* for a very long time." she said making sure they understood the friendship aspect, and she thought of just how far back they went. Once they were happy children playing in the tourist-filled courtyards of Lucca. His family's door was open to her as hers was to him. But Marco wasn't the same as he was back then. There was no loyalty in this man. He claimed and took, but no longer believed in what was right. It sickened her to see the women she loved swoon at his Italian charm.

Russell was the first one to come in from the other room, and he stopped in his tracks when he saw Gia and then Marco with his arm around her.

Glenda moved to him. "Russ, this is Gia's friend from Italy, Marco."

Marco released her to shake Russell's hand. "It is nice to meet you."

"Likewise," Russell said with a glance her direction.

Though she kept her smile in place, she hoped her pleading eyes alerted him to the fact that this wasn't as it looked.

Glenda gathered everyone and moved them all to the dining room. Gia helped carry dishes of food out and set them down before she sat next to Marco, who stood and pulled her chair out for her.

Oh, he was going to give the Walkers a show. She could only pray that none of this made it back to Dane.

As the meal continued, the Walkers seemed to be taken by Marco's charm. Who wouldn't be? He was charismatic and handsome—and sly.

"The bread," Glenda said mid conversation as she realized she'd forgotten to put it out.

"I'll get it," Gia offered as she stood from the table to take a moment to herself.

She walked back to the kitchen, found the baskets of rolls and turned to see Russell standing there, his hands held out to take a basket.

His eyes were focused on her and his lips tight. "Who is he?" he asked, his voice low.

"An old friend."

"An old friend who just happens to show up?"

Gia nodded. "Yes."

He didn't believe her, and it was there in his eyes. "What happened to Dane, and don't feed me any crap about you not seeing him because you don't want to get between us. I know you met up in New York. And I know the man is in love with you so why are you…"

"He is what?"

"I know you're seeing Dane."

"No, that part about how you know he is in love with me?"

Russell took the basket out of her hands and set it on the counter, then took her hands in his. "You're not seeing this man?"

"No. He just showed up, and Bethany thought this was a good idea. I do not want to make a scene. We were old friends. We have a past. But it is the past."

"You have a past? You were together once?"

Gia gave his hands a squeeze. "He comes from good people. In his heart, he is a good person."

"But he hurt you."

"I am just emotional right now. I seem to be a bit homesick. I plan to head back to Italy earlier than planned. His surprise visit has just shaken me up a bit."

Russell kept his eyes on hers. "You're okay, though? This man won't hurt you?"

"No. He would never hurt me," she said, knowing that meant physically.

"And you and Dane?"

Gia smiled as she thought of Russell's words. "Does he really feel that way about me?"

"Who wouldn't?" He lifted her hand to his lips and pressed a kiss to the back of it. "If you ever need me…"

She lifted to her toes and kissed his cheek. "Thank you."

The rest of Thanksgiving dinner wasn't so bad once Russell shared the news he had about Dane. Did he actually think Dane was in love with her?

Even alone in her bedroom, the thought made her cheeks heat.

Marco had graciously left dinner earlier than she thought he might, but he'd sprinkled his charm on the Walkers.

Gia spent the rest of the evening on the computer making her flight plans and talking over plans with Sunshine and Pearl. They would cover her store, and she would leave in the morning for Italy. She'd stay until after Christmas and then she'd return to Georgia and see how things progressed with Dane.

Just the thought of him brought a smile to her lips. Russell's words repeated in her mind, *and I know the man is in love with you.* Maybe she should book her flight for Ohio instead of Italy.

She laughed as she folded a sweater and placed it in her suitcase. No. Right now she needed her mother, her father, and to cuddle on that new baby. Family was more important that thinking a man might love her. Family was her stability—just as it was Dane's. He'd truly understand her need for this trip if Russell was right about Dane's feelings.

Chapter Eighteen

Dishes rattled in the back seat. Not that he had a lot of dishes. In fact, he had a lot of nothing.

Optimism was never his strongest asset. So clearly, having been fired made it seem like this was the end of everything, when in reality, in his heart, he'd never been happier to drive over that Georgia state line.

He should drive right back to his parent's house and settle in. He should start looking for a job. Everything else would fall into place. But instead, he was driving right into town to see Gia. At this moment, he was damn sure she was the only person who could fix his self-doubt. Knowing he was back home should change everything for them. They could finally start being *them*.

Dane parked his car around the back of the building his cousin and her husband owned. They'd done a lot of work on it even since Bethany's wedding.

Tyson stood on a ladder outside of Pearl's bridal store. "Hey!" he shouted down. "Didn't expect to see you around here."

Dane made sure to smile when he looked up at him. "Got fired. Came home."

"Are you handy at all? I'll hire you on the spot to do some work here. I still have to run my own business," he snorted. "This seems to be eating up all my time."

Dane gave it only a moment's thought. "I'd be happy to. I'm efficient in everything but electric. You don't want me touching anything electric."

Tyson came down the ladder chuckling. "I'd leave that to the real professionals. I'm not touching it either." He landed his feet on the ground and wiped his hands with a rag in his pocket. "Why don't you come by tomorrow and I'll get you set up. You'd be doing me a huge favor. And I know you have better skills than handyman work. But…"

"I'm happy to help out. Besides, maybe doing some manual labor will help me move out of the funk I'm in. Hadn't anticipated being unemployed."

"It usually comes as a surprise." Tyson's brows drew together. "What are you doing here anyway?"

Dane couldn't help the smile that surfaced. "I came to see Gia."

Tyson nodded slowly. "Right. I heard you guys were friendly. But I don't think she's there."

"Oh." Dane hadn't considered that. "I guess I'll come back by later."

"No. I mean she went back to Italy."

Now Dane was indeed deflated. "Italy? She wasn't supposed to go back until Christmas."

Tyson shrugged and tucked the rag back in his pocket. "All I know is that Bethany invited some old friend of hers to Thanksgiving, and they left for Italy the next day."

"Some old friend?"

Tyson ran his tongue over his teeth, a sure sign that maybe he was rethinking having said anything. "Some guy who came to see her. An old friend. Good lookin' Italian guy, according to Pearl. I thought he was average at best."

Dane swallowed hard. "And she left with him?"

Tyson gripped the ladder and began to fold it up. "I know she left the next morning, and he was gone too. Sunshine is working for Gia. She might know more."

Dane thanked Tyson for the impending job and headed to Gia's store with a heavy heart.

As Dane walked through the door, the chime above it alerted Sunshine of his presence. She smiled at him as he walked through the door.

"Hey, Dane," she greeted him. Perhaps that's why they liked having her around, she knew everyone by name, even if he wasn't sure they'd met more than once or twice.

"Hi."

"You're looking for Gia?" she asked, clasping her hands in front of her.

"I am. But Tyson said she'd gone back to Italy?"

Sunshine nodded. "I think she was getting a little homesick. I'm sure she'll call once she lands. She didn't want to leave the store once the holiday season started, but when home calls…"

"You go," he finished her thought. "Tyson said she left with a friend?"

Sunshine's forehead creased. "A friend?"

"A man who came to visit?"

Her expression changed considerably, and he'd certainly have thought she was mad. "I don't think she left with him if you want my opinion. I don't think she likes him at all."

That certainly confused him. "Then why did he come to visit?"

She shrugged. "He brought some items for consignment from Lucca. I think they have some past, but I certainly wouldn't say she went home with him."

That certainly did soften the blow, he thought. "Maybe she'll call."

Now Sunshine smiled. "Maybe she will. In fact, I know she will. Should I tell her you were here if I see her?"

Dane shook his head. "Nah, I wanted to surprise her. Guess the surprise was on me." He tucked his hands into his front pockets and rocked back on his heels. "I'll call her later. I'll see you tomorrow. I promised Tyson I'd help out around here with some of the finishing touches."

"It looks beautiful, doesn't it?"

"Who knew a run down building could be spruced up so much?"

"Beauty is always in the eye of the beholder."

Dane nodded. "So they say."

He gave Sunshine a wave and left the store. His mood had shifted slightly, knowing that maybe Gia hadn't run off with some man. Still, it hurt to know she wasn't there. He needed her to be there.

~*~

Gia rested her head against the back of the seat. She'd flown to New Jersey, where she'd had nearly a six-hour layover. They were only an hour into the flight to Italy, so she had plenty of time to relax before she returned home.

The man next to her unbuckled his seat belt and walked toward the restroom. She turned her head to look out the window at the darkness outside.

"I think these airplanes get nicer every year."

Gia turned the moment she heard Marco's voice and watched him sit down next to her and fasten the seatbelt around him.

"What are you doing here?"

"Heading home. Just like you."

She grit her teeth. "I did not know you were on this flight. And that is someone's seat. You cannot sit there."

Marco adjusted into the seat, resting his head back.

"It 's incredible what you can arrange with a first class ticket."

"That does not give you right just to sit in someone's seat."

He grinned. "We traded."

Gia let out a low groan. "Why are you doing this?"

"I would much rather sit with an old friend than the man who was seated next to me."

"Old friend. I do not think we could be considered friends."

"Gia, you hurt my feelings. We have always been friends."

She clasped her hands in her lap. "Friends do not stab each other in the back," she growled. "Which you have been doing since you arrived in America. Only adding to what you have already done."

He nodded. "We have some things to work through."

That had her sitting forward in her seat. "Some things to work through? Marco, we have nothing to say to one another. You hurt me. You...you..." she sat back in her seat. "You are too late," she murmured. "I do not love you anymore. I have moved on."

"You moved away."

"To move on," she whispered. She took a deep breath. It was evident she was stuck with this man for the next six hours. She might as well calm down. Her fate and her future were in her hands. She didn't need to fall into his charm or his traps. She'd done that, continuously, since she was a young girl

When the flight attendant came around with drinks, Marco immediately ordered them drinks, then turned to her with a grin. "You still like mimosas, correct?"

She didn't answer, and she only turned her head to look out the dark window.

"Do you remember the time we were in Venice? We sat on the balcony of the hotel and sipped mimosas."

Of course she remembered that. He'd proposed to her that night—and she'd accepted.

"Why do you bring that up?" she asked, her head still turned from him.

"It is a beautiful memory," he said as the flight attendant returned with their drinks. "*Grazie*," she heard him thank the woman.

He held out her drink, and Gia took it from him. She despised that he knew her as well as he did.

"Let us toast," he leaned in. "To us."

"No," she protested. "There is no us and has not been an us for a very long…"

He held up a finger to stop her. "To us. To new beginnings as friends."

She narrowed her gaze on him, but it had been so long since she had spent time with him, she no longer knew what his true motive was. There was a clarity in his eyes, not the usual sensual darkness.

"As friends?"

He nodded and tapped her plastic cup to his. "As friends, Gia."

She studied him. Looking at him she realized she'd missed him—as a friend. They'd been friends much longer than they'd ever been lovers. What would it hurt?

She tapped her cup to his. "As friends."

But the moment she lifted her cup to her lips, Dane came to mind. She wished it was him she was sharing this moment with.

Soon, she thought as the drink passed through her lips.

Chapter Nineteen

Dirt roads held no secrets. The moment Dane pulled into his parents' driveway, his mother was already headed toward him.

As soon as he parked and stepped out of his car, his mother was there wrapping her arms around him.

"Oh, you're here. I'm so glad to see you. Are you hungry?" She stepped back and looked at him. "You look hungry. Come in and I'll make you something."

Dane smiled and breathed in the affection his mother shed on him. "You knew I was coming?"

"You know. Tyson mentioned it to Pearl who called Eric…"

"Who called you."

"Something like that." She held his stare for a moment. "You're okay? I mean about your job?"

He shrugged. "I was miserable. It was time for me to come home anyway. Tyson offered me some handyman work until I get a job."

She put her hands on his shoulders and smiled at him just as she always would when she was proud of him. "C'mon, let's go inside."

He followed her inside the house and to the kitchen. One thing Dane knew for sure, Glenda Walker wasn't done talking to him.

She pulled down two glasses from the cupboard as he sat on a stool at the kitchen island. She filled each glass with sweet tea and pushed one toward him as she continued to pull items out of the refrigerator to make him a sandwich.

There was a process in everything his mother did. When she wanted information, she got it. And when she wanted to make him a sandwich, she did—and then she started in on getting her information.

"You didn't come home first," she said as she set the sandwiches she'd made on the counter and sat down on the stool next to him.

"I stopped in town. You're right," he admitted as he picked up his sandwich, which she'd cut into triangles.

"You stopped to see Gia."

Keeping his eyes diverted to his plate, he couldn't help but smile. Nothing passed by his mother.

"I did stop to see her, but she's not there."

His mother rested her arms on the island and leaned in. "She went back to Italy?"

"That's what Sunshine said."

His mother nodded. "Did she leave with Marco?"

Now the man had a name, and that didn't sit well with him. "I suppose that's who she left with. I don't know."

"Bethany invited him to Thanksgiving, but I'm not sure Gia was happy to see him."

"Sunshine thought the same thing."

His mother sat up straighter, folding her hands in her lap. "Don't get me wrong. He was a nice man. Very pleasant, but she didn't seem comfortable around him."

Unease spread through him. "There must have been a reason she went back with him, I suppose."

"So she did go back with him?"

Dane shrugged. "I only know she went back. Sunshine didn't seem to think they were together," which he hoped was right, especially after the weekend they'd shared. If she were involved with another man, Dane was sure she wouldn't have let him hold her or kiss her as he had. And of course she wasn't the type to make love to a man and then run away with another—or so he hoped she wasn't.

His mother rested her hand on his arm. "You've always wanted to travel," she said with a warm smile. "You should visit Italy."

"Why would I do that?"

"Because you love Gia."

He narrowed his gaze on his mother, whose lips grew into a tight smile. "I've never said that to you. Why would you think that?"

Her smile widened. "I'm your mother. I've see how you are around her. I watched you collect eggs and dance at weddings. I know you met her in New York. And I know..."

"Mom, I get it," he mused as he felt the heat pool in his cheeks.

She eased back. "She needed to go home. I think she was homesick."

"She wanted to see her brother's baby too."

"If Marco did go back with her, I'm sure she could use a friend from her Georgia home to keep her company."

Dane took another bite of his sandwich before pushing the plate away. "I don't have a job. I can't just jump on a plane and go to Italy."

She reached her hands to his cheeks and cupped his face. "Let me send you to Italy."

"Why would you do that?"

"Because I love Gia too."

How could he possibly pass up the opportunity? "If you insist."

She kissed his cheeks. "I insist."

And he was glad she had. He hadn't known he could miss a woman as much as he missed Gia. He just hoped it wouldn't be too late, and she'd already forgotten about him.

~*~

Gia felt a hand on her shoulder, and she realized she'd fallen asleep. Then she realized she'd fallen asleep on Marco's shoulder.

"We are landing," he whispered as he stroked her hair away from her face. "You have been sleeping for hours."

Embarrassment squeezed at her insides. "I am sorry."

"No, I was happy that you felt comfortable enough to rest on me. Like old times."

That certainly hadn't been the case, and she didn't like that he thought she'd done it on purpose. Travel made her tired, and the mimosa hadn't helped.

Marco adjusted in his seat as if to fix his outfit since she'd been laying up against him. "I also called your father before we took off and told him that I would see that you got home. No need for him to drive to Pisa to get you."

The anger stirred in her again. The chill she'd felt from the recycled air in the plane was now replaced by the heat of her blood pumping through her at a quickened pace.

"Why did you do that? I did not ask you to be my guide. I can get home."

"I am going to Lucca. It is not a problem."

She turned from him, closed her eyes, and wrapped her arms around herself. One ride. She would take the ride from him, but that was it. Marco was infamous for stepping in her way, but she had gotten away from that and for years had made her own way. She wasn't going to let that revert just because he said so. No, she was done with his demanding ways.

As soon as they landed, Gia made her way off of the airplane and to the restroom. She needed a moment to collect herself before she took her sour mood home to her family.

She looked in the mirror and nearly didn't recognize herself. The woman who had looked back at her for the past few weeks had had some hope in her eyes. But today, she looked tired and angry. And why shouldn't she be? She'd lost a lot of sleep since Marco walked into her store and then showed up at dinner with the Walkers.

That was another thing. What might they think of her now? Had Russell made it clear to them that she didn't have an interest in Marco? Or when she got home would they all have turned against her—especially Dane?

She let out a breath as she stroked her fingers through her hair to brush out some of the kinks. She missed him. His voice, his smile, his touch. When she sucked in a breath again, it caught in her chest. Regret was a horrible thing, and now she regretted heading to Italy and not to Ohio.

Right now, she'd give anything to be wrapped in his arms and covered in his kisses.

Gia made quick work of putting herself back together, even adding a bit of color to her lips. She then went to find Marco.

He was standing at the baggage claim looking at his watch. "If they do not hurry we will be late."

"I was not aware we had somewhere to be."

He growled and then moved in when he saw their bags begin to descend. A moment later he had each of their bags and nodded toward the door. She followed as she would have years earlier.

"I can take my bag," she urged as she tried to catch up to him.

"I have it."

"Marco, there is no need for you to…"

"And there is no need for you to argue with me. This is what friends do for one another." Again, he threw that friend word out there.

She followed him out of the airport, and as soon as they hit the air, Gia felt the tears burn her throat. She was home.

Marco turned as he heard her sniff. "You are alright?"

"I am fine. I just realized I am home."

"Do you do this each time you come home?"

Now she could laugh. "Yes, of course, I do. There is no feeling quite like it."

"Then you should stay," he stopped as he approached his car. "There is no reason you should go back to America."

"My life is in America. In Georgia."

"With that Walker family?" His voice had dipped into a tone she was very familiar with.

"Yes, with that Walker family. You had no right to move in on them like…"

He held up his hand to protest her. "They were very kind. I offer them no ill will."

She wasn't so sure of that.

Gia watched as he maneuvered the bags into his Fiat. He then opened the door for her, and she climbed inside. If only Dane could see how crowded the small car was, but how it fit into the city, he would understand why she had to drive one back in America. Perhaps someday he'd see.

Marco climbed into the car, which was no small task for a man of his height. She promised herself she wouldn't laugh. Instead, she rested her hands in her lap and watched as the airport disappeared behind them and the land of Tuscany opened before them.

Chapter Twenty

When Dane had finished his sandwich, his mother hurried about to clean it all up, dismissing his offer to help.

"C'mon, let's go check out flights," she said as she scurried off to his father's office down the hall.

Dane followed chuckling to himself. "You don't have to do this. I know she'll be home soon, and I'm certainly not going anywhere."

She stopped as she cornered his father's desk. "You're going to tell me you can wait for her? It doesn't bother you that some man came from Italy for her? You should talk to Russ. He has other thoughts about it all."

Dane moved toward the desk. "You didn't tell me that."

His mother fisted her hands on her hips. "Listen, there is something about that Marco that doesn't sit right. I don't' know who he was in her past, but she's not comfortable around him."

"And that came from Russ?"

"Yes."

Dane ran his tongue over his teeth. "Why didn't he just go after her then?" He moved to the chair in front of the desk and gripped the back of it.

"Why? What's up with Russ and Gia?" she asked as if she'd never seen a hint of admiration in Russell's eyes.

"Nothing."

"I didn't think so." She sat down at her father's computer. "Now. Can you fly into Lucca?"

Dane shrugged. "How would I know? You're the one who's been to Italy. I've been to Ohio."

"And New York," she said with a grin, but her eyes diverted to the screen.

After some searching, she had found him a flight that left New York on Wednesday. He would stay for the night and fly out Thursday, landing in Pisa on Friday.

"International travel, and you can't even get out of the country for two days?" His remark was snarky, though he'd thought it was in humor until he heard it. Perhaps he was more agitated about it than he thought.

"You could wait for her to come home after Christmas." His mother's voice held the same snark as his had.

He could, but he certainly didn't want to. "I can stand a few days of travel."

"Good. Why don't you call her and tell her you're coming?"

There were many problems with that. First, his cell phone had been his employer's. It hadn't even crossed his mind to take the data out of it before handing it back to them. Now he had one more expense on his plate—a new phone. Being unemployed was expensive.

"I'll talk to Sunshine tomorrow, and she can get me in touch."

His mother finalized the travel plans and printed out the paperwork. "If you tell her your plans, she can at least meet you at the airport."

Dane nodded in agreement as he pulled the papers off the printer and looked them over. The only problem he was foreseeing was, what if she didn't want to see him at all?

There were multiple sides to this trip. His mother was paying for him to travel the world. His wanderlust had never been explored. If everything went as planned, he'd not only see the world, but he'd have the woman of his dreams by his side.

However, if it all crashed around him, he could potentially find himself in a beautiful country, alone. But the more he heard about the man that had come for Gia he felt compelled to seek out some answers. She could tell him it wasn't his place to butt in, but then again, maybe he'd be the right distraction.

Either way, it had been too long since he'd seen her, talked to her—touched her. A part of him felt as thought it had died the moment she'd left New York. Dane needed to make this trip, and his mother had just made that happen. Glenda Walker did love to do everything she could to help fate along when it came to her children and their love lives.

~*~

Luckily, the drive from Pisa to Lucca was a quick one. Gia wasn't much into wanting more conversation with Marco.

Emotion stirred in her and brought tears to her eyes when they turned, and she could see the walls of Lucca. The large arches in the walls welcomed them in, and her stomach began to flutter with anticipation of nearly being home.

This wasn't something new. From the moment she moved away from her parents' home, she'd become emotional at the sight of the walls. As they drove through and entered the city the emotions, she tried to push down flooded her.

Though the sky was gray, and the temperature chilled, there were still people on the streets and running atop the walls.

Gia's heart swelled knowing she was home. There was no place like home—except maybe Georgia and the promise Dane's arms.

Marco's speed slowed as he maneuvered through the small streets and down the back alleys to the parking area adjacent to the building where her family lived.

There was a childlike enthusiasm that filtered through her, and it was as if she couldn't climb from the car fast enough to get upstairs.

Marco walked to the back of the car and lifted the hatch. "Go. I will get your bag."

She'd been hell bent on arguing him at every turn, but now, she was grateful. His generosity would buy her those few precious moments to run up the stairs.

Gia hurried to the door that would lead to the staircase and up to the apartment where she'd grown up.

Her mother waited for her in the open doorway, and a kitchen towel draped over her shoulder and an apron covered her dress.

She held her arms out to Gia and wrapped her in a hug which had the tears that had pooled up spilling over and running down her cheeks.

"Mama," she said as she held onto the petite woman who could mend all her fears and celebrate her happiness.

"Gia, I have missed you."

"I have missed you too." The Italian flowed from her lips.

Her mother looked her over from head to toe. "You are skinny. I made dinner."

"Mama, I thought you were in Rome with Gino," Gia said as she walked into the kitchen and saw her brother standing there.

The tears which had subsided flowed again as she moved to him and he pulled her close for a moment and then turned her around. Seated at the table was her sister-in-law holding the baby that she'd been so desperate to meet.

Liliana stood and moved to her. "Aunt Gia, meet Isabella," she said as she handed the baby to her.

Gia blinked away the tears that continued as she looked down at the beautiful baby in her arms.

Her brother moved next to his wife and wrapped his arm around her shoulders. He gave Liliana a small nod, and she smiled.

"Gino and I are happy to have you here. We want to baptize Isabella this week, and we want you to be her godmother."

She hated being such an emotional wreck, but it was hard not to be. "I am honored," she said as Marco walked through the door and set her suitcase down.

Gino moved to Marco with a handshake and a brotherly hug. "Marco will be her godfather."

The happiness of the moment wavered until Isabella cooed in Gia's arms.

Gia moved to the living room and sat down on the sofa with her niece in her arms. She was perfect Gia thought as she placed her finger in Isabella's hand and she took hold.

She could hear Marco and Gino in the other room laughing as they talked. They were as close as brothers, though she would have thought that might have changed when Marco had broken her heart.

She couldn't blame Gino, she supposed. He had his own life to attend to. Liliana had come along, and love had blinded him to anything that might have gone wrong between Marco and Gia. Then came marriage and babies. Gia wasn't a priority to her brother. The problem had been that she wasn't one to Marco anymore either.

Isabella opened her eyes and looked up at Gia. Her heart melted into goo, just as it had when she'd held her niece and her nephew when they were infants as well.

Marco walked into the living room and sat down right next to her. "She is beautiful."

"She is perfect," Gia admired Isabella, and her heart nearly burst with love for the baby.

"I would bet your babies would be equally as beautiful."

She turned her head slightly, realizing just how close Marco was to her as their noses nearly brushed.

"I am sure they will be."

"It is nice to have you home," he said, draping his arm over her shoulders and then running his free hand over Isabella's soft hair. "Godparents. That is a big responsibility."

She wanted to argue and pull from the intimate moment, but her heart wouldn't allow her to. She loved this little girl so much, and she wanted to breathe in every possible moment with her.

What did it matter that Marco would share such an honor with her? At the end of her trip, she would go back to America and Marco wouldn't be there—Dane would.

Chapter Twenty-One

Gia's mother put together a dinner that could have fed an army. Her father, brother, and Marco decided, afterward, on a few drinks down the street at a small pub which was her father's favorite.

Liliana had settled her son and daughter in front of the television with a movie to watch after they had nearly worn Gia out with their games. Liliana then joined Gia and her mother in the kitchen for coffee.

Gia held Isabella in her arms. Her heart was so full of love it could carry her for very long time when she returned to Georgia.

"They will probably fall asleep right there on the sofa," Lilliana laughed as she sat down.

Gia looked at her sister-in-law and wondered how any woman could look as beautiful and as tired all at one time, but Liliana seemed to manage it.

"I can take her and lie her down," she offered to Gia.

Gia shook her head. "No. I'm cherishing every moment of this."

Liliana stirred cream into her coffee. "Marco is very happy to have you back here."

"I am just visiting."

Her mother patted her hand. "There is always room here for you."

"Thank you. I am happy in America. My business is doing very well. My new location is beautiful. And…" she stopped from talking about Dane, though she wasn't sure why. "I look forward to you all coming to visit someday."

Liliana raised her cup to her lips. "I would like that."

Her mother, however, tapped her fingers on the table. "When will you get married and settle down? Even your sister is getting married."

Gia had been a bit disappointed that her sister hadn't come to see her. "Mama, when the time is right, I will settle down."

"You should settle down here, in Lucca."

"I am enjoying my adventure right now."

She could see the battle her mother had over her saying such a thing. And she was very aware of how her mother felt and why.

Her mother would have liked to have had an adventure or two in her life as well, but it hadn't happened like that. Instead, she fell in love with a man, only a few years later, she fell in love with another and married him—Gia's father.

But that was when the chaos of family dynamics got in the way. The man she'd first fallen in love with was Gia's uncle, her father's brother. Her mother was the reason that the two men hadn't spoken in years. It was the very reason she didn't want to get between Russell and Dane. It wouldn't have been fair to them.

They managed past the topic of Gia moving home and ventured into other areas, which pleased her. They talked of the vendors she carried in her store, other items she wanted to add, and they talked about a trip up to Venice to shop.

Gia missed the bond she had with her family, but she quickly realized she had a bond with her "other" family. She'd celebrated milestones in the lives of Pearl, Bethany, and Susan. She'd grown close to Lydia and was getting to know Audrey as well. Her friendships didn't stop with the just the women who surrounded her and supported her. Their husbands and brothers were equally as important in her life--and their cousins.

She could hear her father, Gino, and Marco as they ascended the staircase to the apartment. Her sister quickly jumped up and pulled open the door.

"Quiet. Isabella is sleeping," she scolded, and the three men looked hurt by her words, and then remorseful as they realized how loud they were being.

Gino apologized and swooped in to take Isabella from Gia and carry her to the other room, and Liliana followed.

Her father nodded toward Gia. "Marco would like to talk to you. Outside."

Marco stood by the door. A hesitant smile formed on his lips and she felt an equal scowl on her own.

Gia stood from the table, walked past Marco, and out of the apartment. She hurried down the steps and outside into the street.

Marco followed, but Gia kept walking. Perhaps a nice brisk walk would do her some good.

"He only meant outside. We do not have to go for a jog."

Gia slowed her pace but kept walking. "What do you want to talk about?"

"Your Papa is worried about you," he said as he caught up to her and they walked down the streets of shops which were closed for the night.

"There is no reason for his worry. I am happy in America."

She continued her quickened stride until she passed the church and came to the Piazza San Michelle.

Marco took her arm and stopped her there. The moonlight filled the square with a beautiful glow. It was one of Gia's favorite places, surrounded by the buildings of Lucca and the church, which was also one of the most beautiful landmarks in all of Italy.

"Why do you run from me?" he asked. "I saw it in your eyes the day I came to your store. You were not happy to see me."

"Why should I be?"

"Because we go back a very long way."

"And I have moved on from that."

His hand still lingered on her arm, but the hurt in his eyes had her standing there without moving. "I have made many mistakes. I have taken advantage of you and our relationship." He moved in closer. "I do not want that. I am sorry for what I have done."

They stood toe to toe now. His face was only inches from hers. "Why are you doing this? You know where I stand."

"I am only asking for your forgiveness. Gia, give me a chance, as a friend."

"A friend?"

He raised his hand to her cheek and held it there. "Only a friend."

She waited for him to make another move, but he didn't. He didn't try to kiss her or touch her in any other way. Had he finally learned restraint?

"Only this one time, Marco. As a friend. Nothing more."

"It is all I ask."

There was a small part of her heart that stopped aching in that moment. She'd forgiven him. That was what he'd asked for and it was what she'd done. As long as he kept his promise, she could be his friend. But her heart no longer belonged to him, it belonged to Dane.

The night air suddenly chilled her. She'd been walking so fast she hadn't noticed it was cold. Wrapping her arms around her, she started back home.

Marco pulled his jacket off and placed it over her arms. "You do not have to be brave around me. I would give you the shirt off my back if..."

"This is nice. Thank you," she interrupted. "Would you mind if we walked just a bit more? I have a feeling jet lag will hit in the morning. I want to walk the streets just a bit."

"I would like that."

And so they walked, and it felt right. Perhaps she had missed her friend Marco, but if failed in comparison to the ache inside because she was missing Dane. She should call him. She would call, as soon as she got back and went to her room. At that moment, she needed to hear his voice, but first, she would walk the dark streets of her hometown and breathe in the air she missed so dearly. And she would make nice conversation with the man beside her—her friend.

~*~

Dane could feel shots he'd taken at the bar swim in his stomach. The moment he'd checked in for his international flight, he'd been nearly sick with nerves. He'd never been one to calm his nerves with liquor before, but he wasn't sure he'd had much choice.

Never had he been on a flight as long at the one he was about to take. He was going to land in Italy and know nothing of the lay of the land or how to get around.

He'd promised his mother he'd call Gia, but he hadn't. There was an element of surprise in what he was doing, and he didn't want to ruin it.

Things could go two ways. She'd either see him and run into his arms—which was the desired outcome. Or she'd start cursing at him in Italian and he'd hop right back on that plane and go home.

Either way, he was worked up.

When the flight attendant came by and asked if he'd like a drink, he ordered coffee. The last thing he needed was to be hung over when he arrived.

Dane adjusted the neck pillow, he'd borrowed from his mother, and looked out into the darkness. Though Dane would never consider himself an expert on relationships, he could claim to have had a few. But nothing compared to this one with Gia.

He and Gia had the strangest relationship of all. There'd been flirting, stolen kisses, and one amazing night in New York. Some might consider that no more than a one-night stand, but not Dane.

He wasn't sure he'd ever actually been in love, but when he thought of Gia, he thought that might be what he felt.

It was much too early to consider that. No one could just fall in love.

Then again, wasn't that what happened to his brother Eric? Hadn't his cousin Bethany fallen head over heels in love with her husband Kent when she met him?

Pearl and Tyson had known each other longer. That relationship made more sense.

He shook his head. None of it made sense.

The flight attendant returned with his coffee and a pastry as well. "You looked as though you could use both," her accent was thick like Gia's, and it only made him miss her more.

"I appreciate it. How much longer is the flight?" he asked, now anxious to land.

"Four more hours. Are you there to sightsee and visit Pisa?" she asked.

"Headed to Lucca."

"Beautiful place. I am from Milan. You might add that to your bucket list," she said smiling with pride. "But if you need anything, you just call for me." She gave him a wink and moved on.

The only thing he needed now was for the plane to go faster.

Chapter Twenty-Two

Friendship had its perks. Gia had a bouquet of fresh flowers on her nightstand when she woke late the next morning, compliments of Marco. He'd also invited her lunch.

Though she was mindful of ulterior motives, she thought she would accept his lunch proposal. As godparents to Isabella, they needed to be on common ground.

Gia picked up her phone and searched her messages. Sunshine had sent her the sales totals from the day before and a list of the shipments which had arrived. Bethany had sent her a picture of the wedding gift she'd given them on display in their house.

But there were no messages from Dane.

She had so been looking forward to seeing him at Thanksgiving. It had been a complete disappointment when he wasn't able to be there. And even more so when Marco arrived. But she hadn't heard from him at all.

Deciding that she needed to reach out to him, she pulled up the text box, sent him a text, and then realized what time it was in America. Surely he'd reply when he got it.

For now, she'd get ready, have some late breakfast, and head out to walk the streets of Lucca. She had some business to do, and she wanted to buy Isabella a gift. Later, she'd make sure she talked to Dane. She was missing him terribly. Hearing his voice was what she needed.

Gia showered and brushed out her hair before she dressed. When she walked out to the kitchen, she heard voices from the living room. Her mother's, her sister-in-law's, and Marco's. Did he have to be there all the time? She hadn't come back to Italy to have him around her. She wanted to be with her family, and that didn't seem to be happening.

He was the first to see her standing in the doorway, and he stood to greet her with a hug and a kiss on the cheek.

"*Buongiorno,*" his voice was soft, with that sweetness she once craved from him, but now found she loathed down to her core.

"Good morning," she replied in English, with even the slightest bit of Southern twang.

Humor lit in his eyes. "Did you forget we were to have lunch?"

"It is not lunch time yet. I have errands to run."

"So do I. I would love the company."

Liliana placed Isabella on her shoulder. "My bicycle is in the back. Take it. The basket is big enough for anything you need."

Marco took her hand in his. "Yes, a ride would be nice."

Gia forced a grin and pulled her hand back from his.

Isabella hiccupped, and Gia looked at her sister-in-law who adjusted the baby. "And be at the church at three o'clock," Liliana added. "We will go over the baptism."

Gia smiled at her sister-in-law, though her insides were twisted. Perhaps she'd been wrong to extend her trip.

Marco followed her outside and around the building to where Liliana said her bicycle was. And of course, her brother's bicycle was there too.

Marco checked the tires. "I think we are good to go."

"You are using his bicycle?"

He chuckled as he climbed on. "I sold mine to a Japanese tourist one day for twice the price."

"That does not sound like an honest thing to do."

He shrugged. "My ex-wife left me no choice."

She could only imagine.

She climbed on Liliana's bicycle and took off toward the street leaving Marco to follow.

The thought crossed her mind to head to the top of the wall and ride around the city. Perhaps Marco would tire and want to leave her in peace, but as he passed her, she knew that wasn't going to happen.

In her heart, she knew what she had to do. What would it hurt to give him his day? By the end of it, she would talk to Dane, and Marco would see that she was not in the least interested in him.

Perhaps Marco had read her mind. He headed for the wall and began a ride around its top. He stayed far enough ahead of her that she was able to take in the scenery she'd missed so much. Briefly, she wondered how she'd ever left a place as lovely as Lucca. Then she thought of her store and her friends. She wouldn't have had that in Italy. Family was wonderful, but sometimes they could suffocate as well.

The Walkers didn't do that—at least from the perspective of an outsider.

Each member was left to chase their dreams if they chose—to find love when it came along.

Marco slowed as they rounded to the back side of the city. There was no need for her to wonder what he was doing. He was making a point.

"Do you remember, Gia?"

She swallowed hard. "I remember."

"We snuck out in the middle of the night and made love under that tree."

It had been the riskiest thing Gia had ever done in her life. Perhaps still was. What had they been thinking? They were so young and foolish. In a city like Lucca, people were everywhere. How had they not been caught?

Thinking back on it made her smile. Her heart seemed to push boundaries and keep her mind from making clear choices. Even she and Dane had been foolish in New York. He could have easily lost his job. But she didn't regret it. It had been the most exciting time, which of course had replaced anything she and Marco had ever done.

"I think we should head down to lunch," he said. "There is a little shop, which is newer, and has many baby items we could look at. I think we should buy Isabella a gift that is from both her godparents."

She didn't want to do that, but it did show solidarity.

Gia filled her lungs with the air she'd craved and decided to let go of the hate for one day. She owed that to herself. She'd promised to be his friend, and she was going to try.

"Lead the way," she said as she followed Marco off the wall and back into the city.

~*~

Dane could feel the pressure of the decent and that woke him from the lovely dream he'd been having about New York. He shifted in his seat. Perhaps he'd been thinking a little too in-depth about their night in New York.

Sunlight filled the cabin of the airplane now. He looked at his watch. It was nearly lunchtime in Italy, and his stomach growled.

He might have to find something at the airport or close by.

An hour later, Dane stood at the baggage claim waiting for his suitcase to arrive. He fished in his pocket for the new cell phone he'd bought. Turning it on, he waited to see if there were any messages.

There was no surprise he had a voice message from his mother.

"Dane, you should get this when you land. I talked to Summer, and she gave me Gia's number in Lucca in case you don't get her cell phone. Call her and tell her you're coming. I also called you a car. I know you said you'd be fine, but it's what I could do. Look for someone to pick you up and take you to Lucca. I'm sure you have enough Euro, but your credit card will work there too." Dane chuckled as he listened to his mother go on. She was one to think of everything. That's why he was there. She'd thought enough to send him.

"And Dane," she continued, "I tucked a little something in your suitcase to give to Gia if you want to. You'll know it when you see it. I love you, darling. Call me."

He disconnected the call just as his suitcase arrived. As he pulled it from the carousel, he noticed a man with a sign that said WALKER.

Dane approached the man. "You're looking for Dane Walker?"

The man nodded. "I am Francesco. I will be driving you to Lucca."

The thought that his mother had arranged that warmed him. "Thank you. You wouldn't mind stopping somewhere for something to eat would you? I'm starving."

Francesco laughed and took the suitcase from Dane. "I will make sure you are taken care of."

Dane was grateful for his mother's planning of the driver. Francesco was an excellent tour guide. Dane learned about Pisa as they drove out of the city. He'd enjoyed a quick bite of meats and cheeses that Francesco had procured at a small shop where the couple that owned it spoke no English.

As they neared Lucca, Francesco told him of the walls that were built to keep out the enemies in medieval times.

The very thought was beyond comprehension to Dane. He was very sure he'd never been in a building that was over two hundred years old.

As they drove through an arch in the wall, Dane immediately knew why Gia loved it so much. He was instantly taken by the charm.

The old brick called to him to touch it. Churches rose from nearly every block. He found himself pressed to the car window to take it all in knowing that in just a few moments he would be able to walk among the history of the city.

Dane found himself holding his breath. Was this was brought on a wanderlust in people? It was all so different and he'd yet to even experience it, but it called to him.

"Piccolo Hotel Puccini, right up here," Francesco said as he drove the small car down the narrow road.

He now understood Gia's choice in car. She'd been right. It was just a little bit of home to her.

"Inside they can direct you to restaurants, museums, and churches. We have plenty of churches in Italy and Lucca had her fill," Francesco laughed.

Dane thanked him as he climbed from the car and looked around. Somewhere within the walls of the city was Gia, and his heart rate kicked up a notch just thinking about it.

He checked into the quaint hotel named after a famous resident of the city. The room was nice enough, and he acknowledged that the hotel itself was delightful, but he wasn't there to sit in his room. He wanted to find Gia and even though he had an address, which Sunshine had texted him, it was going to be an adventure.

Before he left his room, he opened his suitcase to find what his mother had slipped into it. Tucked inside his folded shirts was a jewelry box.

He opened it slowly to reveal a necklace with a small gold cross and a tiny diamond. It was familiar to him. It had been his grandmother's. She'd worn it until she'd been put into a nursing home and died a few years later.

His mother hadn't sent the treasured heirloom as a reminder of his grandmother. There was a particular reason behind it. It was to go to Gia, as a gift from him. It was Glenda's way, passed through Dane, to welcome her into their family. Dane also knew it was a gateway for him to make any move necessary to keep her.

That very thought hit him as if he'd had a ton of bricks dropped on him. To keep her meant he'd need to be honest about his feelings for her.

They'd spent very little time tighter, but enough for him to know that a life without Gia wasn't the one he wanted to live.

Perhaps he'd sabotaged his job so that he could return to her.

He thought of Eric when he'd fallen in love with Susan. It happened fast, and the man had turned to mush. Eric wasn't one to let someone get under his skin, but Susan had—just as Gia had his.

This was it. He knew it now that he'd taken inventory of his feelings. This was love. This was what whittled a man down and made him stop focusing on only himself. Dane had flown across the world just to see a woman—to see Gia. Wondering now if she'd care that he was there just wasn't an option. Now he had to find her and declare this love that was gripping his heart so tightly it might burst.

Dane tucked the box into his pocket and headed down to the streets of Lucca to find her armed with an address and a GPS.

Chapter Twenty-Three

Admitting to herself that lunch had been delightful was hard. Even harder was acknowledging that the company outweighed the food.

Making up her mind to let Marco into her life freed her.

He'd made her laugh as he once had. Captivated her with his stories. Mended her heart with an apology and confessed that karma was indeed a bitch as it was his wife who left him for another man.

There should have been some solace in that, but she felt for him, knowing that pain.

They left the restaurant after a few glasses of wine and of course dessert.

Walking their bikes, they headed down the street to the small store Marco had known about to buy Isabella a gift.

"You have checked your cell phone no less that twenty times since we left home. Who are you waiting for?"

Gia looked up from the phone and at Marco. "I have a business to run. Sunshine is sending me updates."

His eyes narrowed. "And business is bad?"

She gasped at that. "No, of course not. Why would you think that?"

"Because you sigh every time you put it away. It is a sigh of disappointment."

Gia tucked her phone back into her bag. She had not feelings for this man, other than past ones. They had agreed to be friends, so she was going to confide in him. It might prove to be a mistake, but she had nothing to lose.

"I am waiting to hear from Dane."

"Walker?"

"Yes."

He nodded as he put the wrapped gift into the basket on the front of his bicycle and pushed it toward the street. "You are in love with this man?"

Love. She contemplated it though she knew there was no need to. "I think I do."

Marco let out a grunt. "Think you do? So why are you here?"

"I needed to come home," she said walking faster to keep up with him. "He lives away from Georgia, and we just do not see each other."

"That will never work."

Gia stopped, and a moment later Marco did as well.

"Who are you to say it will never work?"

He chuckled. "When two people are apart the heart cannot stay true."

"That is spoken from a man whose heart was never true," she argued, climbing on the bike and riding past him.

She rode until she came to the Piazza San Michelle, crowded tourists. Gia slowed and got off the bike as Marco pulled up next to her.

"I have to say I am sorry, how many more times, Gia?"

"Sorry does not mean much. I am in love with another man and yet you take it upon yourself to tell me what will work with my heart and what will not."

"I have seen it," he said climbing off his bike and leaving it on the kickstand to walk toward her. "I have loved you since we were children. That has never gone away."

"Please do not do that." She brushed away the first tear that fell. "I do not feel that way."

He gently touched her arm. "You could learn again."

"Gia!"

She looked up to see her sister in the square waving and running toward them.

Gia let the bike fall to the ground and ran toward her. They wrapped their arms around each other amidst the crowd of people who watched them.

"Ariel!" She let her sister swing her around as she laughed. "I have missed you," she said smiling at her sister.

"I have missed you too. America is much too far away."

And at that very moment, she felt it. "How was Paris?"

"I would have enjoyed it more had I not been looking over my shoulder every moment afraid someone might begin to shoot in a crowd."

Gia wondered if they had all begun to feel that way, no matter where they traveled.

Her sister pulled her in. "But at the top of the Eiffel Tower Palo asked me to marry him."

Gia and her sister jumped up and down as if they were little school girls with a secret. For too long Gia had discredited her sister's love for the man she'd now marry. Perhaps it had been her own petty feelings over love, but she didn't feel that way anymore. She was genuinely happy for her.

"Ariel, I am happy for you."

Ariel leaned in. "Are you really?" she whispered in her ear, and Gia felt the pang of guilt jab into her stomach.

"I truly am."

"Then meet him." Ariel waved for the man on the outskirt of the square to join them. "Palo, this is my big sister Gia."

"I have heard so much about you," he said extending his hand and then turned to see Marco at her side. "Marco!"

The men hugged in a manly embrace with slaps to the back and deep laugher. "Congratulations," Marco said. "It is about time."

"Tell me," Palo laughed. "I did not realize you two had mended your relationship. Marco talks about you nearly as much as your sister does."

Gia felt Marco's arm slip around her waist, and he pulled her in closer.

"We are friends only," she emphasized.

Ariel pulled Gia by the hand to her bike and picked it up from the ground. "How is your store? Tell me all about life in America. I am going to come and visit after we are married. We might honeymoon there. That would be exciting," her sister said as she pushed the bicycle toward the church, through the crowd of nameless faces.

~*~

Surely no one would notice if Dane died in the square. He stood on the outskirts, a cup of coffee in his hand from the shop behind him.

He'd gone to Gia's house, but there was no one there. So he'd walked around the streets.

He'd first seen her and the man ride away from a store with a gift, just one gift. It looked as though they were arguing, so he hadn't moved in. Was that her brother he'd wondered.

Then he'd touched her ever so gently, and that was when Dane felt the first slice through his heart.

When the woman ran to her and embraced her, he knew that was her sister. There was no mistaking the fact. Then the man slid his arm around her, and Dane was sure that slice in his heart had carved an enormous hole, and he just might die among the tourists who spoke German beside him.

He was a very long way from home to die of a broken heart.

Dane watched as they walked to the church and the men followed. A moment later they disappeared inside.

It would be best if he simply went back to his hotel room, made new reservations, and headed home. This certainly wasn't what he'd expected when he'd planned to surprise her.

Looking around, he spotted a trash can. He walked to it and threw his full cup of coffee away.

No, he wasn't going to go home. He was going to wait for her and confront her. There was a need to know why they'd spent that night in New York and the many kisses in between, and she'd come back to Italy for another man. If he was going to hurt this bad, he needed to know why.

Dane paced the piazza and had looked in every window of every shop near the church. He'd studied the church and wondered how that huge wall that made up the front of the church, with a statue at the top, had stood so long without falling. There was no support on the back or sides, only a staircase to the top. He supposed some things were just built to stand the test of time. The walls of Lucca, the buildings inside, and the walls of the many churches—just not the hearts of those who visited.

Gia watched her brother look at his wife as they held their baby in their arms.

The priest talked to them all about what would happen during the baptism. Gia listened carefully as she'd missed the other ceremonies for her niece and nephew.

She watched as her mother corralled her niece and nephew, who, out of boredom, had begun to push and jab one another, much as she and her siblings once had.

No doubt in the Walker home there was taunting and fighting. Well, she thought, she knew that to be true. She'd seen Dane and Russell go after each other in the street.

In one moment she had been sentimental over her brother's family and in another instant she was missing her family of friends back home.

How had it come to that, and when had Lucca ceased to be home?

In that instant, she knew why. It was Dane. She loved him and yet she hadn't spoken to him in nearly a week. He hadn't returned her calls or texted. The thought that maybe Piper wasn't just a neighbor took over her mind and her heart began to squeeze at the pain the thought brought her.

Marco reached for her hand and gave it a squeeze. She looked up at him, and he mouthed the words that asked if she was okay.

There was no answer.

A moment later the priest announced that he would see them tomorrow, and Gia rushed out of the church with Marco close behind.

As she hit the steps out front, Marco grabbed for her arm and pulled her into him.

"What has happened?" he asked as he ran his hand down her hair. "What has made you so upset?"

She took a breath to speak, but what was she to say? That her mind was filled with all sorts of things and none of them made sense? Perhaps her trip needed to end quickly. She had to go back to Georgia. Even if it was to just throw herself back into her work.

Marco cupped her face with his hands. "Take it easy," he said softly and then pressed his lips to hers.

But the thought of even kissing the man had her pushing him back and away just as she heard her name whispered from a few feet away.

She turned and there he was. Dane stood at the bottom of the church steps looking up at her as if she'd scalded him.

"Dane," she wept as she broke free of Marco's hold and ran to him.

Instinctively she wrapped her arms around him and pressed a hard kiss to his lips, but the warmth wasn't there. She needed that warmth.

Pressing her forehead to his, "You are here, in Lucca. Why are you here?"

He lifted his head and looked up toward Marco. "I'm not sure now."

As she followed his line of sight, she saw Marco, his hands in his pockets and his eyes narrowed on them. Then the door to the church opened, and her family filed out. She looked back at Dane.

"Trust me. Come with me."

She took his hand and headed down a street and across to another and yet another. She weaved them through the city until Dane finally pulled her back.

"Stop. Where are you going?"

"Away from all of them. I want a moment to be alone with you."

Dane looked around them. "I think you've managed that."

Gia turned and reached for his face in her hands. She just wanted to look at him, but he took her hands and abruptly lowered them.

"Gia, what's going on?"

"You are here. You are here with me." She jumped at him and wrapped her arms around his neck. "I have missed you."

Dane eased back. "It didn't look like you were missing me at all."

His voice was sharp, and she didn't like it. "Dane…"

"I saw you riding together and his arm around you when you talked to your sister."

"You were spying on me?"

"Spying? No. I came to find you, but no one was home. Gia, this place isn't very big. It's no surprise you walked right in front of me. But if you have something to say to me, now is a good time."

That was her opening. She would say what she felt. "I love you."

He didn't respond in the way she'd hoped. He only stood there shaking his head. "No, I don't think you do. I love you, and that's why I'm here."

Gia stepped back and fisted her hands on her hips. "You think I do not love you? Dane, I have been calling you and texting you. I had Thanksgiving with your family without you…"

"And you brought him along."

She raised her hand to slap him, but he caught her wrist. "Anger isn't your strong suit."

She wasn't sure what that meant, but she pulled her hand back and waited for another turn to hit the man. Now she understood Russell's rage.

"I did not invite Marco to dinner. I did not invite him to Georgia. He is not part of my life anymore."

"You could have fooled me."

"And I suppose you make it a habit to let your neighbors sleep in your apartment."

"Ex-neighbor, and yes, if they need my help."

That wasn't what she'd expected at all.

"Well…I…" She stopped and studied his face. "Ex-neighbor. I assume she moved out?"

"No, I did," he said tucking his hands into his pockets as if he were trying to keep them from touching her.

"You…why?"

"I got fired. I live with my parents now."

Gia moved toward him, and he took a step back. "You moved *back home*?"

"I did."

She wanted to pull him in and celebrate the moment, but he kept his distance. "Dane, we can be together now," she said pleading.

"I'm not sure that's what we should do. Gia, I don't know you. I thought I did, but…"

She felt the rage start up in her again. "You want to think that I have done something wrong. You are filling your head with thoughts that I raced back here with Marco."

"You seem to know a lot of what's going on in my mind."

"Well, you are wrong. And if you can stand there and think that I would be with a man who broke my heart and left me for another woman, you are an idiot."

"You seem to be still hung up on Piper, and I only let her stay until her mother arrived with the key."

She took a breath to argue and then let it out. "I did that."

"You sure did. And I didn't kiss her or hug her or any of the things I've witnessed you doing in the past hour."

Gia turned from him. "He wants me back. I do not want him. I do not want pain like that ever again."

"Seems you're hurting now."

"Only because the man I love doubts me. He came all this way, and he doubts me." She turned back. "Why did you come all this way to see me?"

"My mother sent me."

"I am sorry she seemed to have made a mistake."

Something in his eyes flickered, and his face softened. "My mother never makes mistakes."

Once he said those words, he pulled his hands from his pockets and moved to her swiftly taking her into his arms and bringing his mouth to hers.

Dane didn't want to be mad, and he didn't want to hurt her.

He'd seen the way she looked at Marco when they'd left the store and how she'd pushed him away when he moved into kiss her. Those weren't the actions of a woman who gave up her shot at love and went back to an old lover.

Besides, she'd said she'd tried to call and text him. Damn, he should have taken those contacts with him when he got a new phone.

When a tour group came upon them, Gia took his hand and pulled him back down the street.

"Where are you staying?"

His mind suddenly went blank. He had to fish for the name. "Puccini something."

The smile was full on her face. "I know the one. It is not far from my home. I want to go back there, to the hotel."

She led him by the hand back to the hotel.

This was more like it he thought as she pulled him through the front door and then let him take the lead up to his room. As he dug the key from his pocket, she wrapped her arms around him and pressed kisses to the back of his neck.

Holding onto the key was becoming a chore, her breath on his neck had his hands twitching to touch her, and it was making it very hard to unlock the door. When he'd pushed it open, he picked her up, carried her over the threshold and straight to the bed as the door slammed shut behind them.

There were no words between them. What would they have said that they weren't showing each other with their hands and lips?

New York seemed to have been too long ago. The desire between them had ignited into an inferno and words would just get in the way.

She pulled at his shirt as he pulled at hers, all the while their mouths stayed connected and the beating of their hearts synced.

By the time she was naked beneath him, he was out of breath, staring down at her beautiful face.

Suddenly the words he'd traveled thousands of miles to say surfaced.

"I love you, Gia," he said causing her to pull him closer again. The rest of the night words would come and go and love making would carry them through the hours. But the genuinely satisfied look in her eyes when he said the words would carry him for the rest of his life.

Chapter Twenty-Four

Dane listened to Gia breath against his chest. She'd nodded off. Who could blame her? They'd been at each other for hours.

His eternal clock had yet to reset, though he'd heard of the curse of jetlag and he wondered when it would hit.

He caressed her bare shoulder, and her hair sprayed across his chest. This was right where he wanted to be for the rest of his life.

Gia stirred. "Did I fall asleep?"

"Yes," he said brushing her hair from her face. "It's okay, though. Rest if you need to."

She lifted her head to look at him. "I'm starving."

"I was hoping you might be. I didn't even pack snacks for the flight. I have nothing to offer."

Gia rolled on her back. "This is where America wins my devotion. We could order a pizza and someone would bring it to us."

"Are we too late to eat?"

She sat up, taking the sheet with her for cover. Pushing her hair over her shoulder, she considered for a moment and then shook her head. "I know of a place we can go, and I can guarantee my parents will not find us there."

"Are we hiding from your parents?"

She pulled the sheet tighter to her. "No. I just need some time."

Dane sat up and touched her arm. "Do they want to meet me?"

A crease formed between her brows which told him a lot.

"They do not know about you, yet."

"Oh, I think they do. They watched us run off together."

That made her laugh, though he wasn't sure why. He'd thought it was a bit terrifying the way she'd zig-zagged through the streets to get away from them.

"I suppose you are right. I will talk to them. Come on. I want to eat."

"Where are we going."

Her lips pursed. "I will explain when we get there."

They'd dressed and now walked in silence, hand in hand, down the dimly lit streets of Lucca. Dane hadn't asked any further questions. He'd hoped that his declaration of love was enough for her to know he trusted her.

She stopped outside a restaurant. "This is it."

"Not very big."

"Nothing here is," she said as she pushed open the door and walked inside.

A man and a woman stood at the back of the restaurant. The woman was picking up plates to deliver to a table, and the man cooked just beyond her. When Gia and Dane walked in, they both stopped and simply stared at them.

He felt her hand squeeze his as the woman nodded to a table in the corner and Gia led them there.

Dane pulled out her chair and waited for her to sit down before taking the seat next to her, but as soon as he sat, Gia jumped up.

The woman who had been serving the dishes took Gia into her arms and began to weep.

Gia comforted the woman in Italian as Dane stood. He wasn't sure what else to do.

The woman pulled back and looked Gia over from head to toe before the man came from the back and scooped her up into his arms as well.

The words began to fly between the three of them, but not one of them made sense to him. But it was obvious they had missed her, whoever they were.

Suddenly they all three turned to him, and he saw the tears that welled in Gia's eyes.

"Dane, this is my aunt Aurora and my uncle Lorenzo."

Lorenzo held his hand out to Dane, and he stepped forward to shake it.

"It's nice to meet you, sir."

He smiled and nodded then said something to Gia in Italian, and she smiled.

Aurora moved to him and placed a kiss on each of his cheeks and then cupped his face in her hands. She whispered something in Italian before smiling at him and moving back to stand by her husband.

They walked away, their arms wrapped around one another and Gia smiled wide.

"She thinks you are handsome, and I am a very lucky girl."

"I think you're lucky too." He winked and held her chair as she sat back down.

"They are going to make us something and then join us when they close up."

"You haven't seen them in a long time, have you?"

Gia clasped her hands together and set them on her lap. "I have not seen them in ten years."

"But you haven't been in Georgia that long."

She shook her head. "No. Lorenzo is my father's brother. They have not spoken since before I was born."

Dane leaned in over the table. "You seem close to them. How does that work?"

"My mother. She and Aurora became friends. Truly that is a sign of the character of Aurora."

"How's that?"

Gia licked her lips and swallowed. "My uncle was once in love with my mother."

Dane sat back in his chair and folded his arms in front of him. "And that was why you were so adamant about Russell and I not seeing you?"

"Yes. It has been so hard to watch them avoid each other my entire life. They live only four streets apart. This city is not that big. Paths cross daily. How can they still not speak?" she said throwing her hands in the air. "But Aurora went to my mother, and they became friends. She did not want their children to be strangers."

"She's a very wise woman."

"That she is."

Gia's heart was full as she walked out of the restaurant, her fingers intertwined with Dane's. Her aunt and uncle had fed them and embraced them. Perhaps in time, she could get her father to talk to him. It had always been a wish of hers that they would do so.

"Can I walk you back home?" Dane asked as they strolled the quiet streets.

"I am going back to your hotel with you."

He stopped and gathered her hands in his. "Are you sure about that?"

Gia lifted her arms and wrapped them around his neck. "I am sure. I am a grown woman and even though I am home, I make my own decisions."

"Are you going to introduce me to them?"

Her eyes diverted to the ground before she looked at him. "Yes, of course."

"Why are you unsure of that?"

She dropped her arms and took his hand, walking quicker than they had been. "I am unsure how they will accept you."

"Does it matter?"

She stopped. "Of course, it does."

"Looks like we hit another wall."

Gia shook her head. "No. This will not be a block. I love you, Dane, and they will too. It is just…" she trailed off, unsure of how to explain it to him.

"Marco? They want you to be with him?" he asked as the very thought sickened him.

"Once. Maybe." She let out a sigh, perhaps it was a cry trying to escape. "Marco seems to think there is a chance for us. He thinks I could fall back in love with him."

"And could you?"

"No," she answered quickly. "He hurt me. That kind of hurt does not go away."

Dane ran his hands over her shoulders and held her arms. "I would never do that to you, Gia. You have my word on that."

She batted her eyes as she could feel the tears sting them. "I believe that. I have been around your family. I know how you were raised."

He pulled her closer to him. "Are you sure you want to go back with me?"

"I am sure. Tomorrow my niece is being baptized. I am her godmother and Marco is her godfather. I hate to throw you into the the fire pit, but…"

"I'll be there, Gia. I love you. Love means that I tolerate uncomfortable family events. It means I stand by your side even when you don't want to be there. It means I trust your heart. If you say you don't love Marco, I believe you, because you told me you loved me."

"I do love you."

"That's all that matters." Dane placed a kiss atop her head. "Let's go back to my room then. Tomorrow we will go to the church for the baptism. After that, whatever you want to do I'll do."

In her heart she knew she could ask for anything and he'd deliver it to her. For now, all she wanted was his courage. Tomorrow was going to be very stressful for them all.

Chapter Twenty-Five

Gia opened the door to her parents' home and walked inside. She could hear her mother in the kitchen moving about. She sucked in a breath of courage and went in.

"Gia!" Her mother quickly moved to her and examined her. "Are you alright? Where have you been? You had me sick with worry all night."

"Mama, I am fine. And you look well rested to me," she said examining her mother's eyes.

"Marco is not happy that you left with some man."

"I do not care what Marco thinks or feels at all. I am not part of Marco's life and I am not sure where he got the idea that I might be."

Her mother fisted her hands on her hips. "Marco is good for you. He made some mistakes, but he would treat you well."

"Mama, I am in love with someone else."

Her mother bit down on her bottom lip. "American?"

"Yes, of course."

"So then you will stay in America?"

Gia folded her arms in front of her in defiance. "Is this what this is all about? If I come home and happen to fall in love with Marco again, I will move back?"

"You do not belong that far away from us."

"I belong where I am accepted."

"You are accepted here."

"I want to be my own person, and I do that in America." She took her mother's hands in hers. "Mama, I am very successful at what I do. My store is very popular. I have friends—dear friends. I belong there."

"Gia, you have all moved away. I have no one here now."

"That is what happens when you have children."

Her mother pulled her in. "I miss you, Gia."

"Then come and visit. Bring Papa and visit me. See what I have built." She leaned in close to her mother's ear. "Auntie and Uncle are coming to America in the spring to see me. You should come with them. You and Papa," she whispered.

Her mother pulled back. "You visited them?"

"Last night with Dane."

"Dane?"

"Yes, the man I left the church with."

Her mother nodded slowly. "And you took him to visit your aunt and uncle and not your parents?"

That stung she thought. "You will meet him today."

"Your papa will not be happy about that, Gia. It is his blessing you need, not his brother's."

"Mama, I didn't go for Uncle's blessing. And I would love to have Papa's blessing, but I love Dane and even if I do not have his blessing, I will still love Dane."

Her mother turned from her and walked toward the cupboard. She took down two cups and poured coffee in them. "Let us go sit on the balcony and watch the city wake."

Gia felt the warmth in the invitation. It had been something she and her mother had always done together.

She followed her mother as she walked through the living room, gathering up two blankets, and then out to the small balcony. She set her coffee on the small table and draped the blankets over the chairs as she would when Gia lived there. Gia sat in one chair and her mother in the other. Each of them wrapped the blankets around themselves to fight off the early morning chill.

"Ariel is getting married," her mother said looking out over the railing. "She told us last night."

"I know. He proposed to her in Paris."

"You never cared much for Palo she said."

That had been childish, Gia admitted to herself. "I never knew him. I felt as though she was being foolish to run off with him and travel."

That caused her mother to laugh. "And she thought you were foolish for traveling so far and settling in America."

They both chuckled. "I guess we always think we know what is right for everyone else."

"Especially when we care for someone." Her mother sipped her coffee. "Where is this man of yours right now?"

Gia sat back in her chair. "I left him sleeping. I needed to get my clothes."

"Tell me about his family."

The very thought of them brought a smile to Gia's mouth. "You would love them, Mama. He has four brothers. They own a ranch. His parents are married and his mother reminds me of you. She loves to take care of everyone."

"She takes care of you?"

"Even before any of this happened with Dane. Even Marco had dinner with them."

"He told us."

"If I had to choose a family other than my own to be with, I would choose them, Mama."

Her mother reached for Gia's hand and held it tightly. "I want your happiness. Your father wants your happiness too, but he would like it closer to home."

Gia nodded. "I understand. Promise me you will come visit me and see why I love where I am at. Lucca will always be home, but so will Georgia."

Her mother squeezed her hand. "Bring him to the church with you."

"He will be coming with me."

"Good. I look forward to meeting the man who has your heart."

Gia loved her mother so much. It sometimes was hard to think about leaving her when she would visit.

Gia opened the door to the hotel room quietly, but the bed was empty. She set her suitcase down on the floor and shut the door quietly.

A moment later, Dane walked out of the bathroom, a towel wrapped around his waist and drying his hair with another.

"How did it go?" he asked as if he knew where she'd been.

"How did what go?"

He smiled. "You weren't here when I woke up. I assumed you went home."

"Just to get my clothes."

Dane dropped the towel he was using on his hair on the bed. "You didn't talk to anyone?"

Perhaps he knew her better than she thought he did. "I talked to my mother. We had coffee and watched the sunrise on the balcony, just as we used to."

He moved to her and took her hands. "Good. She's okay with everything?"

"She looks forward to meeting you. I told her you would be at the church."

Dane lifted her hands to his lips. "Good. By the way, Sunshine called. You sold out of that Venetian glass."

"She called you?"

"You left your phone."

She hadn't even realized it. "Then I shall purchase more."

He pulled her to him, wrapping his arms around her waist. "That means you'll need to travel to Venice?"

"It sounds like it does."

"I've never been to Venice."

Gia lifted on her toes and placed a kiss on his lips. "Mr. Walker, before you go home you will become a world traveler."

~*~

Gia couldn't remember a time when she'd been more nervous. Walking hand in hand down the street to the church, she was sure she might throw up.

"I think we should leave for Venice tonight," she said. "It's only a few hours away."

"You can drive to Venice?"

She laughed. "You can drive to a port and take a boat."

"My image of Venice is skewed by tourist photos. I assume there are only gondolas and people singing."

Gia hugged his arm. "I think you will pleasantly surprised when you see it. And while we are there, we will take a boat out to Burano and buy lace as well. I want to take some back to your mother."

"She would love that."

"I know," she said with enthusiasm, but it quickly faded as they came upon the church. "I guess this is it. Are you ready to meet my family?"

"And Marco?"

She let out a groan. "Yes, and Marco."

Dane took her hands in his. "Are you going back to Georgia with me?"

"Yes."

"Then Marco isn't my concern."

Gia raised herself to kiss him gently on the lips. "In case I forget later, I love you. Thank you for coming to Lucca."

"And I love you. Thank my mother for sending me."

"I will."

Chapter Twenty-Six

Gia and Dane walked through the doors of the church holding hands. Her family was gathered in the back and of course Marco too.

His eyes flashed in anger, which she'd seen many times, but Marco was a professional when it came to putting on a good face.

He moved directly toward them, and even though she was holding another man's hand, Marco leaned in and kissed Gia on the cheek.

"*Buongiorno*, Gia."

"*Buongiorno*."

"Who is your friend?" he asked shifting his eyes to Dane.

"Marco this is Dane Walker."

Dane released her hand and extended it toward Marco. "Nice to meet you," he said.

Marco returned the gesture and turned his attention back to Gia. "I think they are ready."

Dane kissed Gia's other cheek. "I will sit back here."

She watched the men exchange glances once again, and she wondered if they had boxing gloves if they might use them. Though seeing how Dane and Russell had gone after one another in the street, she was sure that he and Marco wouldn't need gloves either.

Dane sat down, and Gia moved to her family.

Her mother smiled as she watched her walk toward her. "Is that him?" She nodded toward Dane.

"Yea, Mama. After the ceremony, I will introduce you."

Her mother touched her cheek. "You look happy."

"I am."

The priest approached them and from then on the morning belonged to Isabella.

Dane watched the ceremony begin as tourists walked in and out of the church quietly. He was fascinated by the steep traditions and orchestrated ways in which the baptism moved.

The steady look Marco kept on Gia hadn't gone unnoticed either.

He sat back in the pew and thought of how badly things could have gone had he not approached her yesterday. Had he taken his thoughts back to America with him, he'd have written her off assuming she was in love with Marco.

He wasn't sure of Marco's true intentions, but he figured they'd made it clear that she wasn't interested.

Isabella slept through her ceremony, even as she was passed from person to person. But when Gia held her, Dane's heart nearly exploded in his chest.

How, in that instant, had she become even more beautiful?

There had always been the thought that someday he'd meet a woman, settle down, and have children. However, seeing her with her niece in her arms ramped the idea to the top of his list.

Dane thought of the necklace his mother had given him to give to her. Perhaps it would be romantic to give it to her when they visited Venice.

He wouldn't give it to her as a gift of engagement, maybe just promise. They were a long way from that final commitment, he decided, though he knew in his heart she was the one. How could he not know when his body reacted to her in so many ways physically and emotionally.

As the ceremony ended and the family walked toward the back of the church, Dane stood. This was the moment. The moment when her father would shake his hand, and he would know the true feelings of the man.

Gia moved right to his side and took his hand. "Mama, Papa, this is Dane Walker."

She spoke in English, which surprised him. Her parents took a moment to process the words and then her mother moved in and kissed him on the cheeks, just as her aunt had.

With her hands lingering on his face she said, "Dane, so nice to meet you."

"It's nice to meet you as well."

As her mother stepped back, her father held his hand out to him. "Dane."

He was harder to read. "It's an honor to meet you, sir."

Her father had locked eyes with him, and Dane kept his mind about him. He was sizing him up, and he knew the drill. This wasn't the first time he'd met the father of a woman he knew intimately.

Gia went on to introduce him to her sister and her fiancée, her brother and his wife, and of course Isabella and her siblings.

Marco stood close by and kept a steely eye on them.

"We are going to eat and celebrate. Then I will tell them we are leaving for Venice tonight."

"I should check out of my room then."

She nodded. "After lunch."

~*~

Before lunch finished, Dane excused himself and returned to the hotel. He made a point to call his mother and tell her how things were going and of his plans.

"Venice is very romantic, Dane."

He chuckled as he packed his clothes in the open suitcase he'd laid on the bed. "I hope so. I think I'm going to give her Grandma's necklace while we are there."

"That's beautiful," she said as she sniffed.

"Are you crying?"

"Oh, hush. I was giving up on all of you. Thank goodness Susan happened into our lives when she did, or Eric would have died a lonely old man."

"I'm not as old as Eric," he teased. "I wasn't a lost cause yet."

"Yet. I knew Gia was something special when I met her."

So did he. "I think I'd like to stay here, with her, until she's ready to go back to Georgia after Christmas. Is that a problem?"

"Not with me," she said. "Do you think she can stay away from her store that long? She's dedicated to it."

"She might not be there physically, but she's working. That's why we're going to Venice. She's placing orders and Sunshine has been in touch with her every day."

"Good. Give her my love."

"I will. Love you."

"Love you too, son."

As he disconnected the call and threw the phone on the bed, he thought he'd have punched anyone who called him a mama's boy, but the truth stung a bit. He was a mama's boy. He didn't remember being so dependent on her, but he was.

She knew him as no one else in the world did. She could get her way too.

The thought struck him that without her he wouldn't be in Italy with the woman he loved. In fact, he wouldn't even know Gia if it weren't for his mother's specific requests to be in the right places at the right times.

Dane was pulled from his thoughts when the door opened, and Gia slammed it behind her.

Her cheeks were red, and her fists balled at her side. There was no need to ask if anything happened at lunch, he knew his answer, so he waited for her to tell him.

"I am ready. Are you ready?"

Dane stood silent for a moment before nodding. "I'm all set. Do we have a car?"

She narrowed her gaze on him. "At this point, we will take the train. I am not asking anyone for anything." Her arms flew about, and her accent had deepened.

Dane moved to her and took her hands. "What happened?"

She began to rattle off words in Italian and her hands broke free of his as she used them to emphasize her words. There was no doubt if this relationship was going to work he was going to have to learn Italian.

Gia stopped and took a deep breath. "Sorry. I got worked up." She paced the room as she collected her thoughts. "My father asked me when I was going to marry Marco. As if he did not notice that I introduced him to another man."

"What did you tell him?"

"Nothing. I did not have to say a word. My mother put him in his place and let him know I did not love Marco." She sat on the bed and took a breath. Then she jumped right back up and paced again. "Then Marco said I would come to my senses. He said that my store was small and unsuccessful, and I would have to leave America soon."

He was sure that was what had pissed her off the most.

"Your mother is okay with us?"

"Oh, she has us married off and having six babies."

Dane choked on his breath. "Six?"

She waved her hand about. "Just a number, Dane. Not for real."

"I'm okay with it," he said, and he saw the fury in her eyes diffuse a bit.

She let out a little hum. "The point is Marco's ego is being fed by my father. Who does that to a person? Who makes them marry someone they do not love?"

"Gia, he can't make you marry him."

"No. He cannot. And I will not. And I never wanted to in the first place."

He narrowed his gaze on her. "You were engaged."

"To a liar."

"Still."

She crossed her arms in front of her. "Dane Walker, what are your trying to prove."

"I'm just saying you loved him once. Your father is confused."

She nodded her head slowly. "Why would you want to be part of a family where the father only accepts his way? I mean, look at his family. He will not talk to my uncle. Does he not realize he won that battle? My mother chose him."

Dane moved to her and placed his hand on her cheek. "And you chose me."

"There was no choice, Dane. From the moment I met you in Pearl's store..."

"I know." He pressed a soft kiss to her lips. "I can talk to your father if you'd like. Let him know my intentions."

Gia licked her lips. "What are your intentions?"

"I don't know really. I know I love you and from that grows great respect. And when you love someone you want them around always and forever."

"Do you see us together like that? Forever?"

"I do."

"And you would have six babies with me?" she asked with a giggle.

"I would," he answered without hesitation.

Gia sighed. "Dane, that is all I need to know. I am not sorry you lost your job."

He laughed and pulled her in. "I'm not either. Who knew that was exactly what I needed?"

"Let us go. My mother is staying with my aunt and uncle tonight. She is too mad to go home with my father. Perhaps when we return the situation will have diffused."

"Isn't that only going to piss your father off more if she stays with them?"

"I think that's the point."

Chapter Twenty-Seven

Saint Mark's Square would forever hold a unique place in Gia's heart. She had bought her first pieces for her store just down one of the side streets. Hand blown glass, she remembered. The pieces sold at her grand opening. She wasn't so sure one of the vases hadn't been purchased by Dane's mother.

"This is amazing," Dane said as he stood in the square and watched the people and birds mingle.

"Your wallet is in your front pocket, right?"

"You told me to do so. I took your word."

She gave him a nod. "Tourist traps bring out the worst in people. But I have heard you get that at Disneyland too."

Dane laughed. "I can't imagine having your pockets picked at Disneyland."

"No. You would just think you lost your wallet on a ride."

He laughed. "I suppose you have a point. I'll consider a new wallet that only fits in my front pocket from now on."

She'd taken his hand and begun their journey down the streets of Venice. There were two specific stores she wanted to visit before they retired to their hotel room.

In the wee hours of the morning, Dane rolled over and saw Gia standing by the window looking out over the canal. She was deep in thought and hadn't even noticed him climb from bed and walk to her.

When he wrapped his arms around her waist, she jumped and stifled the yelp that nearly escaped.

"I did not know you were there."

"I know," he said, pressing a kiss to her neck. "You're thinking a little too hard. What's going on?"

"I was thinking of my store and my shelves. I have an ad for Christmas going out next week. Sunshine said she had a few requests for food items."

Dane gathered her hair and pushed it over her other shoulder, then returned to kissing her neck until she leaned back against him.

"Is that all you're thinking about?"

"No," she cooed. "I was thinking about us."

"That's more like it. Were you thinking good thoughts?"

She turned in his arms and rested her hands on his chest. "What would happen if I changed my mind about living in America some day? I do not see it happening, but what if…"

"We'd move."

She leaned back and looked him in the eye. "Just like that?"

"We'd discuss it, of course," he said placing his hand on her cheek. "But, Gia, I'd follow you anywhere."

She rested her head on his chest. "No one has ever considered me like that before."

"Then they didn't love you as I do."

Gia took his hand from her cheek and placed a kiss in his palm. "I keep telling myself that this is going too fast. How is it possible to fall in love and talk about forever when I have not known you that long?"

"My mother would tell you it's fate."

"I love your mother. I think she is very wise."

"She is." Dane took her hand and pulled her back toward the bed. "C'mon. Let's go back to bed. You promised me gelato on some island tomorrow."

Gia giggled as she hopped onto the bed and Dane lowered himself atop of her.

"Burano. We are going to Burano tomorrow to buy lace."

"Lace, right," he whispered as he pressed a kiss to her neck and followed her collar bone to her shoulder and then over her chest.

She said nothing else. For the rest of the night, there were no more plans made—only love.

~*~

Dane wished he'd traveled more in his life because he looked like a fool with his mouth open every time Gia took him somewhere new.

Burano was breathtaking. The houses were all different colors, and the cobblestone streets were quiet. No cars and hardly any people.

She'd gone into a little shop where the woman was making lace, and they made some business deal they both seemed happy with.

The shopkeeper boxed up pieces for Gia, then kissed her cheeks before they left.

"What just happened there?" he asked as they walked on.

"I ordered some items for the store, and I have some very nice handkerchiefs for not only your mother but your cousins too. And I got one for Lydia and one for Sunshine."

"You're very thoughtful."

"I am blessed to have two families. My family here and my family in America, who understand me better than my blood family."

Dane stopped and turned toward her. "Is that what you consider all of us? Family?"

"Of course. You have all been there for me."

His mouth went dry. "I've been saving this because I didn't know if there would be a right time."

He put his hand in his pocket and Gia's eyes went wide. "What are you doing?"

"My mother sent this with me." He opened the box, and Gia batted her eyes when she saw the necklace. "It was my grandmother's. She wanted me to give it to you."

"Me? This is your family's. It is an heirloom."

"Yeah." He pulled it from the case. "I get that now. Now I understand why she wanted you to have it." He held it up to her.

Gia turned and pulled her hair over her shoulder to expose her neck.

Dane slipped the necklace in front of her and latched it in the back. He then took her by the shoulders and turned her toward him. "She thinks of you as family too. I think of you as family."

She touched the cross pendant with her fingertips. "So what does this mean?"

He chuckled. "I don't know really, but maybe it's a good place to start. Gia, let's consider it a promise—not a proposal. But will you promise to think about forever with me?"

Her smile was wide, and her eyes were damp. "Of course—yes."

"Six kids? All with a wanderlust for locations like this?" He lifted his hand to reference the beauty of the local far from home.

"Yes," she laughed as she fell into his arms. "You make me very happy, Dane Walker."

"No, but I think I will."

~*~

Gia's head rested on Dane's shoulder as the train passed through the Tuscan countryside. She found herself reaching for the cross often, just to feel it. There was something powerful in owning an item that meant a great deal to someone else. Especially when that person was Dane's grandmother. And to think Glenda wanted her to have it.

By the time they made it back to Lucca, it was late, and they hadn't made reservations to stay in a hotel. There were only two choices. Home or her aunt and uncle's.

"I'll go with you, wherever you choose," Dane said, standing in the street holding their luggage.

Gia looked up at the home she'd cherished and now fretted. "I think we will go inside. I have not talked to my mother, but something tells me by the darkness of the house, she is not here."

"Lead the way."

Gia opened the door that led to the stairs. She hesitated, then started her journey toward the front door. When she pushed it open, the apartment was quiet. A soft light in the living room was the only light on.

She softly walked toward it. Dane set the suitcases by the door and followed.

Her father sat alone in his chair, a glass of wine in his hand.

"She is not here, Gia." His voice growled and cracked.

"I cannot blame her."

Her father let out a grunt as she moved to him.

She looked down and studied him. He was unshaven, and shadows darkened his eyes. "Have you moved in two days?"

"Why bother?"

"This does not sound like you at all. Papa, what is wrong?"

He lifted his eyes to her, and she saw the tears that welled in them. Gia knelt down before him, and he reached out to touch her hair.

"You look just like your mother when I met her."

"You have told me that before," she said.

"My brother loved her first. He wanted to marry her."

"I know," she admitted.

"Gia, I stole her away. What kind of man does that to his brother?"

"Papa," she reached up and cupped his scruffy cheeks. "She wouldn't have gone had she not loved you. She is my mother. She would not marry a man she did not love."

The tears finally fell from her father's eyes and he set his glass on the small table by his side. "I was wrong to send Marco to you. I thought you would love him again and come home."

Gia rose on her knees and wrapped her arms around her father. "Oh, Papa. I do not love him. I love Dane, and when I am with him, I am home."

She eased back and watched as her father wiped tears from his cheeks. Gia stood as her father rose from his chair and looked at Dane.

"You love my daughter?" he asked in broken English.

Dane stepped further into the room. "Yes, sir. I do."

"You came all this way just to be with her?"

Dane gazed at Gia, and she felt her heartbeat quickened in her chest. "Yes, sir."

Gia's lip began to quiver as her father walked toward him. Her eyes filled with tears as she watched him size him up and then offer his hand and Dane shook it.

"She is my baby, and she will always be my baby. I only want her happy."

"I want the same."

The wall of tears broke free when her father pulled Dane to him and hugged him as a man would hug a son.

Gia covered her mouth with her hand to keep the sobs from escaping.

Her father stepped back, cleared his throat, and wiped his cheeks. "I should go to my wife," he said to Gia.

"You should clean up first," she laughed, and he nodded in agreement. Gia walked to him. "Make amends with Uncle as well. Papa, it has been too long not to speak to your blood. Mama does not want that, she never has."

"Pride, Gia."

"Sometimes you have to let it go."

He kissed her forehead. "You are wise."

The quiet of the apartment was broken when Dane's phone rang. He quickly reached into his pocket to silence it.

Gia watched as his face distorted and he retreated toward the front door to answer.

"Mom?" was all she heard.

She looked at her father. "He is a good man. He comes from a good family," she promised him. "I will be okay."

"A father will always think his daughter's home is with him. We miss you."

Gia moved in and wrapped her arms around the man who would love her always. "I miss you too, Papa. Visit me in America. See what I have built."

Her father kissed the top of her head. "I will."

Dane walked back into the room. His gaze was focused down on his phone before he lifted his head and looked at her. His eyes were wide and his face frozen in a state of panic and confusion.

Gia moved to him. "What is wrong?"

"Russ." He swallowed hard. "That was my mom. Russell was in some kind of accident coming home from Athens. She doesn't know much more than they are headed to the hospital."

"Dane," she moved into him and pulled him into her arms. "We should go. I will make arrangements."

Dane shook his head and placed his hands on her shoulders. "You need to be here. Your family needs you as much as my family needs me," he whispered.

Gia turned to look at her father as he paced the living room. Dane was right, and it broke her heart.

"Will we ever get to be together?"

"Forever, sweetheart."

Chapter Twenty-Eight

The sun painted the sky with yellows and oranges. Gia rested her head against Dane's chest. His arms were wrapped around her as they watched the Tuscan sunrise from the top of the wall that surrounded Lucca.

"Is Paris nice?" he asked softly in her ear.

"It's lovely."

"I think I'd like to see it."

She sighed enjoying the warmth of his breath against her neck. "I always wanted to honeymoon in Paris," she admitted.

"I'll keep that in mind."

Gia turned in his arms. "I am glad Russell is okay."

"So am I. He's going to have a lot of rehabilitation with his leg and hip being fractured. That's not going to go over too well with him."

She raised her hand to his cheek. "He will make you suffer with it."

"Of course, he will. And I'll be there to get him through it. I should be able to make it to Athens before they transport him. Mom sounded pretty shaken up when they took him in for surgery."

"It could have been worse."

"Small miracle, right?"

Dane cupped her face in his hands and locked eyes with her. "Everything here will be okay too," he promised. "Take care of your father. He needs you."

"I will. And I will be back right after Christmas. Perhaps we could celebrate the new year together, and there will be no more being apart."

"I'd like that," he said as a car horn from the street blared. He looked down and waved. "That's my ride."

Dane leaned in and kissed her with such warmth she was sure it pinked her skin. As he pulled away, he touched the pendant on her neck. "It looks good on you."

"The promise looks good on me."

Dane nipped her lips one more time. "I promised you forever, sweetheart. We'll get there."

He picked up his suitcase and headed toward his taxi that waited. Gia fought the urge to run to him and beg him to take him with her. She didn't want to be apart from him ever again. But her dedication to her family kept her feet planted as she watched him load his suitcase into the taxi.

Forever. The word played over and over in her mind until she just couldn't let it go.

"Dane!" she shouted after him as she ran down the incline toward him.

He motioned to the driver to wait a moment and walked toward the base of the wall.

Gia huffed as she came to him and he reached for her.

"Gia…"

"I cannot let you go."

Dane clasped her hands in his. "I have to go. What's wrong?"

She began to laugh. It wasn't the right emotion, but it took over. "Nothing is wrong. I just realized that forever does not have to wait, and I want a bigger promise."

He narrowed his gaze on her, and she was sure he thought she'd gone mad. "What bigger promise?"

"Dane, marry me."

His eye went wide, and his mouth opened. "Gia…"

"Do not try to talk me out of it or say it can wait. I do not want to wait. Dane, marry me. Be my husband forever. And we can live in America and collect eggs in the morning and sell our wares all day. And when a wanderlust takes over we can travel—together. See the world together. Have the world—together."

His hand came to her cheek, but he didn't say anything. Then a smile turned the sides of his mouth up, and she was sure she'd seen the glistening of a tear in his eye.

"I can't think of anything I want more than to be your husband."

Gia jumped up, and Dane swung her around in a circle before setting her back on the ground, and she caught her breath. "I should have asked your father first," she joked.

"He might be disappointed."

They laughed as they pressed their foreheads together and caught their breath.

"Be safe," she intertwined their fingers together and gave his hand a squeeze.

"I will. I have a lot to look forward to."

"I will be home soon," she promised.

"And at that moment, we'll start our forever."

We hope you enjoyed Wanderlust.
Here is an excerpt from the next book in the series.

WALKER REVENGE
Book 5 in the Walker Family Series

Check www.5princebooks.com for buy links
and release dates.

Chapter One ~ Walker Revenge

Daytime TV sucked. If he was subject to one more game show or stupid talk show, Russell thought he might just throw the remote control through the front of the TV.

There was only one upside to being laid up in a hospital bed—not having to work. Though he wasn't sure that this was much consolation.

"You look like crap," his brother's voice came from the doorway.

When Russell turned he saw Dane standing there, but the look on his face wasn't one of humor, as the comment might have suggested. He looked mortified. Russ knew how bad he looked. Hell, you didn't total your truck and walk away without a cut or bruise. Or in his case, you didn't walk away.

"Why'd you leave your vacation so soon?"

"Italy is ugly. Thought this would be a better use of my time." Dane stepped into the room and looked down at the tubes and bandages that encompassed the lower left side of Russell's body. "What the hell happened?"

Russell ran his hand over his stubbly chin, dragging wires tubes along with his hand. "I got pinned in my truck."

"Mom said you flipped it."

Russell puckered his lips. Admitting fault wasn't something he was particularly good at. He was better at dealing with things in a physical manner.

"Hence me getting stuck in the freaking truck."

Dane rubbed his eyes. "I see it did a number on your attitude too."

"Did you come here to fight with me?" He heard his words slur from the crap they'd knocked him out with. Why did that stuff have to stay in a body so long? "What the hell time is it anyway?"

"Six in the morning."

Russell turned off the TV. "And here I thought I was watching crappy daytime TV. I guess it's just always bad." He winced from the pain that seemed to be greater than the pain medicine pumping through his IV. "Why are you here at six in the morning?"

Dane moved to the chair next to the bed. "I flew in and came straight here."

"You left Italy to come here? Dude, I'm sorry."

Dane grinned. Maybe he sounded worse in reality than Russell thought he did in his own head.

"You're sorry? I never thought I'd hear you say that."

"How did it go?" He wasn't in the mood to be jabbed at.

Dane's expression changed and his eyes lit. "It's a beautiful place. It'll be nice when I go back."

"You're going back?"

"Sure we will. That's where Gia is from. Besides, she wants to honeymoon in Paris."

Russell tried to sit up but found it took too much effort. "Honeymoon? What the hell is that supposed to mean?"

"She proposed to me," Dane said, and the smile on his mouth was enormous. The urge to slap it off surged through Russell.

"She proposed to you? You couldn't even do that right?"

Dane shrugged. "You know me. I would have waited too long."

Russell felt the quick fatigue of arguing with his brother begin to take over. He batted his eyes against it.

The next moment he opened his them the room was quiet, faint light pushed through the drawn shade, and a woman stood next to him. He smiled through the haze he was feeling.

She was holding his hand in her hands. Blonde strands of hair hung around her face, but the rest was piled up in a messy bun atop her head.

This was familiar he thought as he took a cleansing breath and then wiggled his nose because his nasal cannula was making it itch.

"I didn't mean to wake you. I was just getting your vitals," her voice was soft and oh so familiar.

"What time is it?" His voice was barely functioning.

"Just past eight."

"I was talking to Dane."

She laughed now, and that too was familiar. "He left hours ago. He looked as though he needed some sleep. Pretty exciting that he's getting married to Gia. I enjoy her store."

That danced around in his head and so did whatever they'd put into his IV, but at least he wasn't in any pain.

"You know Gia?"

"Of course, I do."

Russell lifted his hand, cords and all, and rubbed his eyes. He wasn't seeing clearly, and his mind was beginning to play tricks on him.

Now he turned his head so he could better see the woman in the dimly lit room. Her head was tilted as she focused on reading the monitor at his side, but he knew the curves of her face.

He'd heard that dreams could be vivid when you were on pain meds. Seriously that had to be what was happening.

"Chelsea?" Her name seemed louder when he said it, but she lifted her head.

"Hello, Russ." She went back to looking at the monitor.

"What are you doing here?"

"I went back to school." She lowered his arm back to the bed and then pushed a few buttons on the machine. "How are you feeling?"

"Fine. Confused. You're a nurse?"

"Nursing student. I'm being supervised, so please don't argue with me."

This was no dream. Only Chelsea would ask him not to argue with her. It seemed he'd been willing to fight with everyone.

Russell reached for her, and she quickly glanced out the window used for observation. "What can I do for you, Mr. Walker?"

"Stay for a little bit. I'd like to talk."

"I have rounds to make. I can't spend any time in here talking. If you'd be more comfortable, I could ask to be transferred to another unit."

His world was fuzzy again, but he wasn't done. "No, I don't want that at all. I owe you an apology. I want to give that to you."

She turned to the computer at his bedside, scanned her ID tag, and then entered something with her back turned to the window.

"Russ, I hate to see you in here like this, but something tells me you deserved it."

"That's a horrible thing to say."

She gave him a grunt. "You got in a fight at a bar before you flipped your truck because you'd been drinking."

"I wasn't drunk," he defended.

"Maybe not, but I'll bet your mouth was getting you in trouble, which says to me, nothing has changed." She tucked one of those loose strands of blonde hair behind her ear, a sign that she was nervous. "If you're sincere about talking, I'll come back when my shift is over."

"I'd like that," he said, but his tongue felt as though it filled his mouth and didn't sound right. "I'm sorry," he said slurring his words.

"They gave you something to manage your pain. You will probably sleep a lot."

His eyelids grew heavy again, but he forced them back open. "I love you, Chelsea," he managed before he couldn't lift them open again.

Chelsea focused on the computer screen or pretended to. In her month of internship at the hospital, she'd run into a lot of people she knew. She'd never thought she'd run into Russell Walker, at least not in the shape he was in.

She glanced at him from the corner of her eye. He was smiling in his sleep. And what had made him say that to her? *I love you, Chelsea.* They hadn't spoken in nearly three years. She hadn't seen him since he'd been discharged from the Army.

His mother had invited her to his "Welcome Home" party, but Chelsea hadn't gone. How could she?

She couldn't imagine what he thought he needed to apologize about. After all, she'd been the one to break his heart. She'd been the one to get engaged while he was deployed.

Chelsea squeezed her eyes tightly to ward off any tears that might threaten. The Walkers had raised decent men, even the hot-tempered Russell. He hadn't deserved a two-timer like her.

The head nurse walked into the room. "Everything okay in here?"

"Yes. He woke up for a moment, but the pain meds kicked in."

The head nurse checked her watch. "Okay, you'll come back through in another hour and do this again. His surgery was major, and he'll need to be constantly monitored."

Chelsea nodded as she tucked her pen into her pocket and picked up her paperwork. She would certainly need to ask for a different rotation until he was better. Looking down at his bruised face and his cut up arms broke her heart. But she was sure that wasn't the deep-rooted source of her anguish.

His words were ringing in her ears. Any other day she'd have written them off as banter from a patient on meds. But this was Russell Walker—her first love.

Did he mean what he'd said because she'd never stopped loving him, even after she'd gotten married.

No wonder that hadn't lasted long.

Chelsea walked out of the room and down the hall to her next patient. But for the next hour, all she could think about was Russell Walker and what might have been had she not have been so spiteful and had waited for him to return home.

Meet the Author

Bestselling Author Bernadette Marie is known for building families readers want to be part of. Her series The Keller Family has graced bestseller charts since its release in 2011, along with her other series and single title books. The married mother of five sons promises Happily Ever After always...and says she can write it, because she lives it.

When not writing, Bernadette Marie is shuffling her sons to their many events—mostly hockey—and enjoying the beautiful views of the Colorado Rocky Mountains from her front step. She is also an accomplished martial artist with a second degree black belt in Tang Soo Do.

A chronic entrepreneur, Bernadette Marie opened her own publishing house in 2011, 5 Prince Publishing, so that she could publish the books she liked to write and help make the dreams of other aspiring authors come true too. Bernadette Marie is also the CEO of Illumination Author Events and Services.

Bernadette can be found at:
www.bernadettemarie.com
www.facebook.com/authorbernadettemarie
www.twitter.com/writesromance
info@bernadettemarie.com

Books from 5 Prince Publishing
www.5princebooks.com